Holding hands was different

There was something between us now that hadn't been there—a strong sexual attraction. I could feel it in the dampness of his hand where before it had been dry. I could feel it in the way that just the touch of his hand was now sending signals to the rest of my body. Where before I had found Sam appealing, where before I had appreciated his warmth and his concern and his good nature, now I was finding him amazingly sexy.

There is something about the buildup of sexual tension before you make love for the first time that is never repeated again. Other things take its place, but that initial excitement is never again duplicated. It was the very best of feelings; it was also the most frustrating by far....

ABOUT THE AUTHOR

Beverly Sommers's trademark is humor. And no one writes it quite like she does. Here she tells a comedic tale in the first person, her favorite viewpoint. A lover of travel, Beverly was born in Illinois, lived for a time in California and now makes her home in New York City.

Books by Beverly Sommers

HARLEQUIN AMERICAN ROMANCE

HARLEQUIN INTRIGUE

Don't miss any of our special offers. Write to us at the following address for information on our newest releases.

Harlequin Reader Service
901 Fuhrmann Blvd., P.O. Box 1397, Buffalo, NY 14240
Canadian address: P.O. Box 603,
Fort Erie, Ont. L2A 5X3

GETTING EVEN

BEVERLY
SOMMERS

Harlequin Books

TORONTO • NEW YORK • LONDON
AMSTERDAM • PARIS • SYDNEY • HAMBURG
STOCKHOLM • ATHENS • TOKYO • MILAN

Published October 1989

First printing August 1989

ISBN 0-373-16313-4

Chapter One

It was the summer the beaches died.

It was the summer of the drought, of temperatures over ninety degrees for weeks on end.

It was the summer where the air quality became dangerous; when the city imposed a curfew on Tompkins Square Park and the residents rioted; when fires, raging out of control in Yellowstone National Park, partially blocked out the sun as far east as New York City.

It was the summer my husband left me for my best friend.

I WAS THE RESIDENT REVIEWER of horror films and documentaries for a weekly newspaper called *Views and Reviews*. At *Views* we prided ourselves on seldom agreeing with the *New York Times*. If they were currently extolling the mayor, we were bashing him. If they nominated one movie as best film of the year, you could be sure we'd choose another. It was our managing editor's way of gaining attention and credibility, and once in a while it worked.

It was the day after my husband left me, a Monday, that in my capacity as film reviewer, I arrived late for a screening I was scheduled to see and found the lights already out in the screening room. The film was just beginning as I slid into an aisle seat in the last row.

It would not be exaggerating to say that it wasn't a good day for me. I hadn't slept at all the night before, I was feeling rejected and depressed, and it would have suited me far more to be shown a horror film where I could commiserate with other miserable people. Instead, from what I could garner from the screen, it looked as though I was about to be treated to some dismal study of ants living together happily in the jungle. At the moment I was in no mood to see anyone living happily together, even ants.

I slid down in my seat and rested my head on the back. My view was now partially blocked by the person seated in front of me, but since the top of the screen appeared to be exactly like the bottom of the screen, it didn't seem to matter.

The air-conditioning wasn't working very well, I was dead tired, and the position I was in was conducive to sleep. Not surprisingly my eyelids began to close. I reached down into my carryall and pulled out the thermos of coffee I always sneaked into screenings. It wasn't that I would've minded a nap, but snoring in screenings was not considered professional. A little caffeine might just do the trick.

I unscrewed the top and took a swallow. It was almost too hot to drink and so I left the top off and settled back down with my arm on the arm rest and the thermos in my hand.

The next thing I knew something was waking me up, and the something in question was a yelp from the person sitting beside me as he leaped out of his seat. Then I noticed that my thermos was tilted over in the direction in which his lap must have been a moment ago.

People were turning their heads to see what the trouble was. As my fellow moviegoer sat back down, I whispered, "Did I spill coffee on you?"

"Was it hot?"

"Yes."

"Then I guess that's what you spilled."

"I'm so sorry."

I set the thermos—now empty—down on the floor and rooted around in my bag until I came up with a few tissues.

As he took them from me, the screen got lighter and I got a look at him. I saw the outline of curly hair and beard and the glint of glasses. It was by no means a detailed look, but at least a general outline enough to tell me that forty-eight hours earlier I would have considered him exactly my type. He looked like my husband. He looked like every man I had ever dated. He looked like a lot of men in the city. He had the kind of dark, intellectual look that had always appealed to me. It was the kind of look you see on chess masters, poets and professors in the NYU film department. Having just been dumped by my husband, it was the last look I felt like seeing sitting next to me in a dark screening room. It wasn't rational, but I was almost happy I had spilled hot coffee in his lap. If I couldn't do it to Max, I had at least found a Max lookalike to take my revenge out on.

I settled back in my seat again and looked at the screen. A soothing voice was doing narration and the screen was still full of jungle and crawling little ants. In fact there were so many ants on the screen, they made me itchy. I slid down in my seat and didn't fight it when my eyes once more began to close.

I came awake for the second time when someone nudged my shoulder.

"What is it?" I asked, a little too loudly, getting some disapproving looks from the people in front of me.

"You were falling asleep," whispered the Max clone to my right.

The audience burst out laughing and for a moment I thought they were laughing at what he said. Then I realized how paranoid that sounded and moved as far away from him in my seat as was possible.

He nudged me in the shoulder again. It was a gentle nudge, not the kind where you could call an usher and ask for him to be thrown out.

I glared and him and he said, "You've got to see this next part."

Critics aren't usually told they've "got to see" *anything*, but then he had no reason to think I was a critic. I was still glaring at him, wondering how to get him to leave me alone, when the audience again burst into laughter. I looked at the screen but all I saw were the same ants and they really didn't amuse me.

"You missed it," came his whisper.

I grabbed my bag and pushed my way through the swinging doors and out to the reception area. There was no one around so I lit a cigarette. There had been a time in the not-so-distant-past when we had been allowed to smoke in screenings.

It was cooler in the reception room and the temperature, along with the raised nicotine level, made me think that it would be possible to stay awake for the balance of the film. I had to at least see enough of it to base my review on.

When I went back in I thought of changing seats but it would have necessitated climbing over people, so instead I took my aisle seat again.

Two seconds later I heard him sniffing. "You were smoking."

"Are you going to call the police?" I whispered back.

The same jungle and the same ants were on the screen. The ants seemed to be moving along in a column with a purpose in mind. Not knowing the purpose, I began to amuse myself by counting the ants. Somewhere near one hundred, I fell back asleep.

A coughing fit beside me brought me back awake. Perhaps the smoke from my cigarette had seeped under the door and was even now giving him emphysema. I reached into my bag and found a box of throat lozenges and passed them over to him.

He put one in his mouth, and then murmured. "This isn't candy."

"Why would I be giving you candy?"

He handed the box back to me. "You don't seem to like the film."

"It's pretty hard to get excited about a bunch of ants."

"The ants are a metaphor."

Now he not only looked like my husband, he talked like him. Unfortunately for him I had had enough of film philosophizing to last me the rest of my life.

"Oh, right," I said, managing to put some sarcasm into my whisper.

"I don't think you're giving it a chance."

"I don't have to give it a chance. It has to capture *my* attention, not the other way around."

"I'm sorry," he said.

"You don't have to be sorry. Whoever made this bomb is the one who should be sorry."

After that he didn't wake me up again.

IT WAS ON an overcast, drizzly Wednesday in May that my husband called me from school. "What're you doing this afternoon?" he asked.

This was odd enough in itself; Max never called me during the day. I remember feeling pleased that he had taken the time from his busy teaching schedule to think of me. "I have a screening from one to three," I told him. I had told him the same thing only that morning, but Max never allowed his mind to fill up with unnecessary details that might get in the way of all his brilliant theories.

"Oh," he said, sounding disappointed.

"Why did you want to know?"

"I thought maybe we could eat lunch together."

That would be a first; we never ate lunch together. "I could get away now," I said, not wanting to demolish his expectations. Fool that I was, I was actually excited about the idea of having lunch with my husband.

"I can't. I can't get away until one."

"Maybe tomorrow," I said, but Max had already hung up. Max didn't believe in hellos and good-byes.

When the projector broke down and the screening was postponed until the next day, I arrived home at one forty-five and found Max and my best friend, Jean, chasing each other around the living room, completely naked.

I stood in the doorway, wanting to run and hide. I found myself wishing that I had never seen this, that instead I had stopped for lunch or gone by the office. And then the reality of the situation hit home and I thought, No, *they* should be the ones wishing they were somewhere else.

I didn't even look at Max. I looked at Jean and saw that she couldn't meet my eyes. She wasn't even trying to cover her body, though, and I saw that Jean had cellulite on her thighs and poor muscle tone. Her breasts drooped, but they were large breasts and that might make them a novelty for Max. I briefly wanted to kill her, but even a move toward her on my part would turn what was surely tragedy into farce.

Not knowing what to do or what to say, I went back out and shut the door and went down to a coffee house on Bleecker Street and sat outside at a table and had tea, even though the waiter didn't want to serve me out there in the drizzle. I made myself sit there for thirty minutes while reels of nude shots in Technicolor ran though my head. I made an effort to edit Max out of the pictures, but it didn't work. I played the scene over and over again in my mind. I'd pan the living room, then zoom in for a close-up of Jean's breasts. I'd cross cut between Max and Jean, the final dissolve coming at the sound of the door closing.

By the time I finished my tea I had almost convinced myself that there could be a logical explanation for what I had seen. Other, that is, than the logical explanation that my husband and my best friend had been engaging in something sexual. I started to picture them waiting for me at the apartment, bursting into laughter when I came through the door and explaining the joke to me. Only what kind of joke would necessitate them taking their clothes off? I couldn't conceive of any circumstances under which I'd remove my clothes in front of Jean's husband. And yet she was my friend and he was my husband and there had to be an explanation for what I had seen.

I wasn't sure what to expect when I got home and opened the door, but neither Max nor Jean was still in the apartment. I was so certain they would still be there that now I didn't know what to do. I felt like an intruder in my own home. I wanted to talk to someone about it—but the person I usually talked to was Jean. My mother, who had never warmed up to Max, would tell me to come home to California where I belonged.

I curled up in the overstuffed chair by the window and remembered all the conversations I'd had with Jean. Jean taught poetry at NYU and was always comlaining how bored she was with her husband, Edward, who was a market analyst on Wall Street. I found Edward boring, too. I had a feeling it had been a mistake when I told Jean that Max was never boring, especially in bed.

When Max came back, hours later, I was still sitting in the same place, in the dark, my tears long dried. I thought he would start making excuses to justify his behavior. I had my arguments all prepared, was ready to counter anything he might say, but he didn't say anything at all. He walked past me in the dark, turned on the light in the bedroom, and two minutes later the light was turned off and I heard him get into bed. I wished I had the courage to march into the bedroom, turn on the light, and ask him what the hell was going on. But I didn't. I ended up falling asleep in the chair.

For about two weeks after the incident, Max was home a lot. Up until then I had no idea that his workload at NYU was so light. He started hanging around the apartment, running out only briefly to teach one class or another. I found myself staying out of the apartment more than usual, simply because he was making things impossible at home. He was acting sorry about what he did, but since he refused to discuss it, I didn't know exactly how much he had done. If it was only that one afternoon, I felt I could forgive him. Not Jean, though—I could never forgive Jean. But if it had been more than that afternoon—and I felt sure it was—then I didn't know whether

I was up to forgiving him. I liked my marriage and had always thought it would last forever, but if he had been cheating on me for a long period of time, I knew I'd never be able to trust him again. And while I wasn't someone who liked change, a new life seemed preferable to the old one without trust.

During that time I never once saw Jean. While before we had always been running into each other in the elevator, the laundry room and on the street, now it was as though she had vanished. I needed to talk to her but I didn't want to make the first move. I also thought she should be the one to make the first move. If I had been caught like that with her husband, I surely would have wanted to explain the circumstances as quickly as possible. Not to mention apologize. It seemed that all Jean wanted to do was avoid me.

One day I got up my nerve and called her at a time when she was usually home. She answered the phone and I found I couldn't say a word. After she said hello a few times, I hung up the phone and sat there. I was certain she would know it was me and call back. I sat there for a very long time but she never called me back.

I confronted Max one Sunday afternoon in desperation. I told him that our marriage was obviously over and asked him what he wanted me to do.

Max looked both surprised and baffled. I thought it was the fact that I had said anything at all rather than what I said.

He swore he still loved me but that he needed to get Jean out of his system.

I burst into tears. I hadn't meant to, but I couldn't help it. "I don't know what to do," I told him. "I don't know how to act around you anymore."

"I just need some space," he said.

"I give you space."

"No you don't. You revolve your entire life around me."

"I thought that's what you're supposed to do when you're married."

"I can't take that kind of marriage," he said, although it was the first I'd heard of that in seven years. "Make yourself some friends," he told me. "Get out once in a while."

My crying increased. "Jean was my best friend," I managed to say, the tears dripping off my face and onto my blouse.

"Just give me some space, okay? Let me work through this thing in my own way. I'm not seeing her anymore, if that's what you're worried about. Just don't stay up waiting for me and quit watching me all the time." With that, he reached for his scarf and went storming out the door. He even slammed it behind him, as though I were in some way at fault.

After that I found myself becoming a person I didn't recognize. I waited up for him; I tried to listen in on his phone calls; I even stood across the street from the building where he taught on Washington Square South, waiting for his classes to be over, and then, in the shadows, followed him. I didn't catch him out in anything, but it seemed to satisfy some need I had. Some need to drive myself crazy. And the worst thing was, I found that I missed Jean more than I missed Max. I missed having someone to confide in.

Gradually I stopped following him, stopped searching through his pockets, stopped jumping whenever the phone rang and he went to answer it. Things seemed to be getting back to normal. And then one Friday evening in the last week of May, when I was home alone, someone knocked at the door. When I answered it, it was Edward.

Edward looked distraught. Since he was the kind of person who got distraught over such diverse things as political coups in Haiti and the interest rate rising one half of one percent, I didn't think anything of it.

"Do you want to come in?" I asked him, then remembered that I was no longer speaking to his wife.

It was too late to rescind the invitation because Edward was already in the door and heading for the kitchen. If he thought I was going to offer him a drink, he was wrong.

He sat down in one of the kitchen chairs and slumped over the typewriter. "I suppose you know," he said.

I tried to remember what I had read in the paper that day that could be the cause of Edward's distress. Since he had come to me, I thought it might possibly have something to do with the movie just released about Elvis that some of his fans were picketing because they said it portrayed him as Satanic.

"I had no intention of seeing it anyway," I assured him.

"Seeing what?" Edward asked me.

"That new movie—"

"Movie!" shouted Edward. "Are movies the only thing you ever think about?"

I tried to remember the stories on the front page of the *Times* that morning, but nothing came to mind.

Obviously I was taking too long thinking because Edward finally said, "She's leaving me," then broke down in tears.

"Oh."

"Is that all you can say? I blame Max for this, you know. And I blame you for not keeping Max satisfied."

"Well, she's not leaving him for Max, because Max is—"

"They're together right now, in our apartment. She wants me to pack and move out."

I felt myself falling to pieces and grabbed on to the kitchen table. How could my husband be in another apartment in the same building with another woman without my even suspecting it? Was I as stupid as I felt or had I known all along and refused to believe it? I didn't find either choice acceptable. If I was that stupid, or that desperate, then I wasn't the person I thought I was.

I opened my mouth and screamed, "Well, why are you here, Edward? Why don't you go talk to her?"

"I've been talking to her for months."

"*Months?* This has been going on for *months*?"

"Where've you been, Ellie?"

I realized I'd been in a fantasy world, and one of my own making. "Oh, Edward, we've got to do something."

Edward looked up at me and I didn't like the expression on his face. "Maybe we should have an affair, Ellie, and show them how it feels."

"Forget it!"

"I mean it. What the hell, it can't make things any worse." he got up from the table and started moving toward me.

I turned and ran into the living room, Edward right behind me. When I got to the front door, I opened it wide and said, "Get out of here, Edward, and I mean it!"

Looking disappointed, Edward left.

I didn't know what to do. I tried to tell myself that maybe Jean's throwing Edward out had nothing to do with Max, but then why was Max over at their apartment? And Edward had said "months." Could Max really have been having an affair with her for months?

I was still standing by the door, closed now, wondering about this latest development, when a folded piece of notebook paper came sliding under the door.

I wondered if Edward was on the other side of the door, writing me notes. I didn't want to read it and walked away from the door, but a minute later my curiosity got the better of me and I picked up the paper. As soon as I opened it I recognized Max's erratic handwriting. "Dear Ellie," I read. "I feel I need some time to myself. I'd appreciate it if you'd find your own place this week as I'll be returning next Saturday and at that time I'd like the apartment to myself. Max. P.S. As you know, the lease is in my name."

I felt like storming up the stairs to Jean's apartment and confronting them. I felt like going into the bedroom, gathering up all of Max's clothes, and tossing them out the window. I felt like calling the airlines and making a reservation on the next plane to California. What I didn't feel like doing was crying; by this time I'd cried over Max enough.

I was more interested in trying to figure out how something like this could have happened.

I NEVER FELL in love with the nice, uncomplicated sort of boys I grew up with in California, although I tried. The fair-haired boys with their surfboards tied to the tops of their VW bugs, the laid-back ones who came from suburban ranch houses or beachfront property and ended up going to the University of California and becoming professional men, like my father and brothers, never appealed to me. Instead I fell in love in all the wrong places: in coffee shops with bearded poets, with wild-eyed revolutionaries during political demonstrations, in subway stations, with men waiting on the other side of the platform for trains going in the opposite direction of mine, with Greenpeace daredevils who hung suspended from bridges—but never with anyone who seemed even remotely familiar to me, who in any way reminded me of home.

In my second year at Orange Coast College, I decided I wanted to be a documentary filmmaker. Up until then I was majoring in drama because my best friend, April, was and because it was considered an easy major. I was writing short plays that my teacher kept criticizing as being TV sitcoms, and I had ambitions to direct. In my directing class, though, the actors working on my project would never pay any attention to what I said.

During the Christmas break my boyfriend's older sister came home from New York where she was majoring in film at Columbia University. She had been homecoming queen at our high school the year I was a freshman and I remembered her as tanned and pretty and very popular. She went steady with the captain of the football team. Now she was pale and wore only black: thick turtleneck sweaters, skinny pants, sleek boots, even though the temperature was in the eighties. She drank endless cups of coffee and eschewed the beach. When I told her where I was going to school and that I was majoring in drama, she told me the theater was dead and film was the future. She spoke of Fassbinder's clarity and the director as visionary. She tossed around words such as *film noir* and cinéma vérité. She spoke about a new cinematic language that reconciled the conflict between the exigencies of historical accuracy and the need for artistic creation. She spoke in hushed tones about the solemn simplicity of a pan, the inherent dramatic impact of a close-up, the poignant understatement of a fade-out. I found her fascinating and wanted to be exactly like her. Because of her, Orange Coast College now seemed totally unsophisticated and my boyfriend a bore.

I broke up with my boyfriend and applied to several film schools. I didn't go to UCLA or SC, along with every other aspiring filmmaker in California. Instead I went east to New York University where I believed that the atmosphere was more intellectual and the finished product more artistic, and where I also believed the men would be more to my liking. And I was right on all three counts. What's more, while I had always loved movies, now I fell in love with film.

I roomed with a dark, intense girl named Alicia Quattro, who had lived in New York all her life and had been in analysis for most of it. She dragged me all over the city to little art theaters, where we'd sit through the foreign film twice and then stay up all night analyzing it. We would sit in Village coffee shops over endless cups of espresso, talking about women's role in film and planning the production company we would one day form. We did our student film together, me writing and directing, Alicia doing the camera work and the editing. We got a B on the project and were certain we would've gotten an A if there hadn't been discrimination against women in the film department.

In the two years we roomed together, we became as close as sisters. I spent school holidays with her at her family's weekend house on Long Island, rather than making the long trip to California. We dated very little but went to most of the parties given by other film students, and even had a few of our own.

And then, in my final semester of film school, I fell in love with an intense, bearded intellectual who admired my blond hair, my California clothing and my accentless speech. He was not only more intense than Alicia, he was thought to be the best director in graduate school at the time and his student film won the top award. He seemed to already know everything I aspired to learn and I never tired of hearing him lecture me on the subject of film. Since I couldn't be him, I wanted to belong to him.

Max and Alicia disliked each other from the start. She thought he was overbearing and pompous. He thought she was a dilettante from a rich family who went to film school because it was currently the "in" thing to do. It didn't matter what Alicia thought, though, because I was sure this was the grand passion that I had been waiting for. And the sex with Max was marvelously imaginative.

I was eager to move in with Max Ranier. Instead, and at his insistence, we got married. I kept my own name, which, as it turned out, was the only independent gesture I was to make during seven years of marriage to Max.

Because Max wanted to finish graduate school and he didn't want to have to work at the same time, I took a job as a third-string movie reviewer for a third-rate New York weekly.

Alicia got tears in her eyes when I told her about my first job. "I wish you'd see my shrink," she begged me. "You're throwing away your whole future."

"I'm just postponing it until Max gets his doctorate," I told her.

"That's what they all say," warned Alicia.

"We're going to be different," I assured her.

"I don't even understand what you see in him. Do you ever have fun with him? I've never even heard him laugh."

I wasn't after fun and laughter; I equated fun and laughter with California boys. What I wanted was serious and intense and intellectual. That's what I found sexy.

By the time Max got his doctorate, Alicia was dating a theater major who had inherited the biggest apartment on the Upper West Side that any of us had ever seen. Richard and Max didn't get along so we didn't see much of them socially.

Alicia wouldn't give up. "He'll never let you do anything. Max can't stand competition. You're going to end up a housewife." It was the worst thing either of us could conceive of.

I didn't believe her, though. I pictured me and Max in the future making documentaries together on important subjects. Instead, seven years later—my hair a few shades darker, my clothes and accent having taken on aspects of the big city—I was still reviewing horror movies and obscure documentaries and Max had settled for teaching cinematography at NYU. And Alicia and I hadn't seen each other in years.

Now, of course—after the fact—I wished I had listened to Alicia. If I hadn't married Max, he wouldn't have been able to dump me. He wouldn't have been able to rob me of my best years and then leave me for a woman with larger breasts. Forget her poetic mind—I knew damn well that her mind hadn't been the attraction for Max.

It would have been very easy to crawl into bed and feel sorry for myself. I found, however, that self-pity wasn't high on my emotional list. What was in first place on that list was revenge. Somehow, some way, I was going to hurt Max and Jean the way they had hurt me.

Out of love, I had spent seven years devoting my time and energies to Max's career rather than trying to further my own. I had given dinner parties for his colleagues even though I hated to cook. I had done his laundry, ironed his shirts, picked out birthday presents for his mother, and listened to him talk about himself for seven years, only to have him dump me for another woman.

I had been a good friend to Jean: listening to her endless complaints about Edward, reading her lousy poetry that was only marginally better than the kind you get in cheap greeting cards, walking her dog three times a day whenever they went out of town for the weekend, bringing her food when she was sick, loaning her clothes and cheering her up when she was in one of her moody stages, only to be repaid by having her steal my husband away from me.

If it took me the rest of my life, I was going to get even.

Chapter Two

Review/FILM
THE THING THAT ESCAPED
by Ellie Thomas

Once again we have an average family in small-town U.S.A. with two precocious children. And yet again we have a laboratory experiment that just happens to escape, showing up at the home of young Billy Smith (Michael J. Wolf) and his younger sister, Katie (Polly Ringgold). Written, produced and directed by Gene Finkle, this low-budget effort fails to induce even the slightest gasp of fear in the audience and the "thing" looks like the do-it-yourself effort of a learning-disabled child. Mr. Finkle would have been well advised to allow this movie project to escape.

Rated PG

"HEY, ELLIE," yelled Woody from his office, "could you come in here for a minute?"

"Hi, Woody," I started to say, then noticed he had a window fan in his office. I would've liked one of those but my office—well, a cubicle, really—didn't have a window. I was already feeling sorry for myself and seeing Woody's window fan didn't help. "Aren't they ever going to fix the air-conditioning?" I asked.

"Don't hold your breath," said Woody. "Listen, Ellie, we were talking about you this morning."

What had Max done, called my office and told them he was leaving me? No, that wasn't Max's style. Being paranoid on the subject, though, I couldn't conceive of any other reason my co-workers would have been talking about me.

Woody said, "You know I don't criticize you on your reviews, but the rest of us loved *The Thing*."

It took me a moment to figure out what he was talking about. "You saw it?" I asked.

"I thought it was a *tour de force*—"

"Woody, are we talking about the same movie? *The Thing That Escaped*?"

"The dynamics between the thing and—"

"*Dynamics?* Woody, that was one of the worst movies I've ever had to review, and you've given me some real losers. My seventy-five-year-old grandmother has made better home movies with her video camera."

"Janet Maslin in the *Times* called it 'delightfully original,'" said Woody.

"I really doubt that."

"Here," said Woody, shoving the *Times* across his desk. "Read it. And the *Voice* called it 'hauntingly reminiscent of Spielberg's early efforts.'"

"It was hauntingly reminiscent of a bad dream, the kind you have when you're a kid."

"All right, all right," said Woody, "so we don't agree on this one. It's just that . . . well . . . lately . . ."

"Lately what?"

"Well . . . you seem to be . . ."

"I seem to be what, Woody?"

He backed off from his original query. "Is anything the matter?"

"Is anything the matter with *what*?"

"Never mind, it's none of my business."

"Woody, would you please just tell me what's on your mind?"

"Well, your last few reviews..."

"What about my last few reviews?"

"They haven't seemed to be up to your usual incisive standards."

"You find my reviews incisive?"

"Hell, Ellie—if I didn't, I'd fire you."

"Am I being fired?"

Woody let loose a very long, very disgruntled sigh. "Ellie, baby, no one's being fired."

I was almost disappointed to hear it. I thought of telling Woody I was quitting, but then I thought of having to support myself and I changed my mind. Anyway, no one rents apartments to unemployed people.

"It's not as though you give me Academy Award contenders to review," I told him.

"It's just that... Well, hell, Ellie, if you can't say something nice, can't you at least be funny? You're very funny when you want to be, you know."

"There's nothing funny about a lousy movie."

"You used to think there was. You used to have everyone roaring over your reviews. You write very funny stuff."

"I guess I don't feel very humorous lately."

Woody suddenly broke eye contact. "Since you brought it up, Ellie—"

"I didn't bring anything up, Woody."

"I've noticed—*everyone*'s noticed—you haven't been your usual cheery self lately. At first I figured, well, you know—PMS. But it's been going on for a while now. Is there anything you want to talk to me about?"

The reference to PMS really ticked me off. Woody was the one known for his mood shifts, not me. In fact my moods were steadier than anyone I knew. I always used to be in a good mood; now I was always in a bad one.

I said, "No, there's nothing I want to talk to you about."

"If you want a raise, that's out. If there was anything extra in the budget, I think you'd agree we need some window air conditioners."

I looked pointedly at his new window fan.

Woody looked over his shoulder to see what I was looking at, then gave a sheepish grin. "Listen, I bought that with my own money. If it'll make you happy, take it. Go on, I'm serious. I don't mind sweating."

"You know I don't happen to have a window in my cubicle, Woody."

"Oh, yeah—I forgot about that. Well look, come sit in here anytime you want. Anyway, you got it made—the screening rooms are air-conditioned, aren't they?"

"I'm not complaining about the air-conditioning, Woody."

"Then what are you complaining about?"

"I wasn't the one doing the complaining."

"Oh, yeah. Well, look, you haven't been feeling well lately? Is that it?"

It was going to have to be said sooner or later, and now was as good a time as any. I looked down at his desk. "Max and I split up."

"Speak up. I can't hear you over the noise of that window fan."

I looked up at him. "I said Max and I split up."

"I don't believe it. Not you and Max. Is this a joke, El?"

"It's no joke."

"When did this happen?"

"On Sunday. But things haven't been good for some time."

"How long you been married, ten years?"

"Seven."

"Seven years. That's almost a lifetime. You don't just break up a seven-year marriage."

"I guess Max doesn't know that."

"El, El, what can I say?"

He got up from his desk and walked around to me. Woody-the-concerned-boss was now going into action. "Hey, honey, what can I do to make things easier for you? You want a week off with pay? Yeah, go on, take a week off to get your life sorted out, okay? You haven't taken any vacation time yet this year. Yeah, that'll be just the ticket—take a week off and don't see any movies at all."

I considered his offer for about ten seconds. I could probably use the time to look for an apartment. The problem was, I needed the routine. If I didn't have to go to screenings, I wouldn't have any reason to get up in the morning.

"Thanks, Woody, but I think I'd rather work."

"Yeah, work's the best thing for you. Keep your mind occupied. Hey, I got it! Want to switch a few with George, review a few comedies for a change?"

"I'm not in the mood for comedies," I said.

"Of course you're not, that was a stupid suggestion. Well, look—I'm always here if you need someone to talk to."

"Thanks," I said, although he was probably the last person I would confide in. Talking to Woody about anything personal was the same as taking out an ad in the paper.

He handed me a revised schedule of screenings. I saw that I had one every day and two at night. "All of these are opening this week?" I questioned him.

"You can't handle it?"

"Yeah, I can handle it."

"It's summer, what did you expect? And you're in the middle of that documentary film festival at Columbia. Now get out of here—you got one in an hour. And, El...?"

"Yes?"

"Max wasn't a lot of laughs, anyway."

I SAT IN MY CUBICLE and contemplated my revised schedule. My cubicle was minimalistic: no window, nothing on the walls and only enough room for a typing table and chair. It was also claustrophobic, which was why I wrote my reviews at home. Now that I had to move, however, and since the typewriter at home was legally Max's, I might have to start typing them up at work.

Then I thought, *The hell with that!* Getting revenge on Max and Jean wasn't sitting in a hot, airless cubicle for the rest of the summer. I could start taking my revenge by finding an even better apartment, one with my own office and maybe even a terrace. Max had always been jealous of people who had terraces. I had an instant fantasy of Max arriving at my new apartment and begging me to go back to him. I would look around the apartment, look at Max, and then say, "I don't know, Max. I don't really think I could give up my terrace."

It was a somewhat satisfying fantasy, but the reality was that I was already, after five minutes in the cubicle, soaked with sweat.

I BOUGHT A *TIMES* and a container of coffee and carried them with me to the subway station at Sheridan Square. It was only the beginning of June and already the forecasters were predicting a hot summer. Since it was already eighty-four degrees at ten-thirty in the morning, I had to agree with them.

A woman with a baby in her arms and a small child by her side appeared to be living on the stairs in the subway entrance. The woman asked me for change. I scrounged around in the bottom of my handbag, and came up with sixty-five cents. Other than that, I only had the two twenties I had just gotten out of my bank machine, and I couldn't afford to hand out twenty-dollar bills. Feeling a little guilty for only having sixty-five cents, I also handed the woman the cup of coffee. I had my thermos filled up with decaf since I still hadn't been able to sleep at night.

I bought tokens and headed through the turnstile. Inside the subway station it was several degrees hotter and the air was oppressively close. A young man with a violin was playing Mozart and had already gathered a crowd. I stood there and listened to him until the approaching train drowned him out. I was already sweating when I boarded the car, and the blast of cold air felt wonderful. This year, for the first time that I could remember, all the trains on the Seventh Avenue line were air-conditioned, or at least all the ones I had taken so far.

I stood directly under the air-conditioning vent at the end of the car, holding on to the pole. In front of me a man had passed out and was sleeping it off, curled up on

the seat and smelling of wine. The rush hour was over,
but the train was filled. I heard the door between the cars
open and moved forward a little, to allow whoever was
coming in room, but the person stopped behind me.

"I have AIDS," I heard a voice say, almost in my ear,
"and I've been thrown out of my apartment. I don't have
medical insurance and I was fired from my job." The
voice went on and on.

I tried to tune him out, but I couldn't. Finally, when
the man asked for money, I reached into my pocket and
brought out a subway token and put it in his cup. At the
other end of the car I saw a man in a wheelchair heading
in my direction. He was also talking, but I couldn't hear
what he was saying.

As he got closer, I was able to read the sign hanging
around his neck. In hand-printed letters, it said, "Vietnam Vet, I don't get any government benefits."

I found that I rated panhandlers in much the same way
that I rated movies. Women with children always tugged
at my heart and I always gave to them. The man who said
he had AIDS also got my sympathy. Vietnam vets didn't,
though. First of all, I thought the government should be
taking care of them. And secondly, ever since *Platoon*
had gotten good reviews, they seemed to be everywhere,
as though Charlie Sheen's being in it had somehow vali-
dated the war. This man in the wheelchair was good-
looking and articulate; I didn't know why he couldn't
find a job.

Nevertheless, this particular veteran was now telling his
story once again, and seemed to be telling it to me alone.
I had moved aside so that he could get past me, but he
seemed to be content to tell only me the reasons why he
wasn't getting any government benefits. When he stopped
and eyed me—and I could swear his eyes were laughing

at my predicament—I said, "I'm sorry, I don't have any money." I could feel myself flushing from the lie.

"How about a cigarette?" he asked me.

"Oh, sure," I said, digging down into my carryall for my pack of cigarettes. I held it out to him, and he removed one, then stuck it in his pocket.

The train pulled into Fifty-ninth Street and I got off. As soon as I came out into the daylight I lit a cigarette. Two panhandlers immediately asked me for smokes. I handed my pack around, then lit their cigarettes for them. I got a disapproving glance from a businesswoman who passed by, but I ignored her. I found I would rather hand out cigarettes than money. Some days it seemed that except for the homeless, I was the only one still smoking in the city. I handed out cigarettes just so I wouldn't be the only one.

The screening was at Cornerstone Pictures production offices. The screening room was air-conditioned and only partially filled. I saw Meredith, the reviewer for a teenager magazine, waving to me, and sat down beside her.

"The season begins," said Meredith, alluding to the fact that summer was the season of teenage films.

"What're we seeing?" I asked.

"*Terror at Thomas Jefferson High School, Part Six*," said Meredith.

"Another one?"

"Another one."

"I didn't like the first five," I said.

"Ah, but the kids did."

"Meredith, do you know of any sublets for the summer?"

"Not offhand, but I'll ask around."

"Thanks."

"I thought you were married."

"We're separating."

"It's his apartment?"

I nodded.

"What rotten luck."

The lights began to dim and I got out my notebook and pen and then slid down in the seat. When the room was in total darkness, I closed my eyes and began to think about how unfair my situation was. I was going to be out on the street while Max and Jean were going to have two, two-bedroom, rent-controlled apartments.

The next thing I knew, I was coming awake with a start and Meredith was nudging me.

"What's wrong?" I asked, opening my eyes and seeing the screen still blank. "The projector break down again?"

"You slept through the whole thing," said Meredith.

I sat upright in the seat. "I didn't get any sleep last night."

"Well, you just got a good two hours' worth."

"Did you take notes?"

"Of course I took notes."

"Would you mind—?"

"Only if you buy me lunch."

"Okay, but just tell me one thing. Did I miss anything?"

"A worse piece of trash I never sat through."

"Can I quote you on that?"

"Don't you dare!"

I SAT in Washington Square Park marking the apartments for rent with a yellow marker. So far there was very little yellow showing against the black and white, which was due to the fact that there were very few apartments available, and what there were, were mostly out of my price range.

I knew one thing for sure, and that was I was going to miss Washington Square Park. I was going to miss living in Greenwich Village on a tree-lined street. I was going to miss it because the only way I could afford to live there was if I was married to someone teaching at NYU. On my salary, the only park I could hope to live near was Tompkins Square Park, which was located in what used to be the cheapest section of Manhattan, but was now, so I heard, being gentrified.

My first choice would have been the Village since *Views and Reviews* had its offices there. I wondered if I killed Max whether I could conceivably retain possession of the apartment. I didn't think so. I wondered if I killed Jean whether Max would want me back. That was possible, but in that case I wouldn't want him. I wondered if a handsome, charming man was even now walking through the park and was about to notice me and invite me to move into his nine-room apartment on Sutton Place with him. I looked up, saw only drug dealers and old men playing chess, and decided it wasn't likely.

I saw a shadow fall on my newspaper and looked up to see a well-muscled black man in red jogging shorts.

"You got a cigarette, lady?" he asked.

I wanted to point out to him that jogging while smoking wasn't a good idea, healthwise. Instead I said, "Sorry, but this is my last one."

"Could I have the rest of it?"

I handed over the last inch of my cigarette.

I wondered if I was going to have to give up smoking. It wasn't likely I was going to be able to afford to furnish all the nonpaying smokers with cigarettes much longer.

But now was not the time to quit smoking. Now, consumed with revenge, the last thing I needed was another stress-inducer.

Max and Jean were quite enough.

I WENT HOME to type up my review of *Terror at Thomas Jefferson High School, Part Six*. I'd get that one out of the way so that all I'd have to do when I got home from the film festival at Lincoln Center that night was write the review of the documentary I'd be seeing. Then I'd get up early in the morning and try to find an apartment.

The apartment was ice-cold when I entered it. It felt wonderful. Max had always complained if I didn't turn the air conditioner off whenever I left the apartment. He said he was into conserving electricity. The real reason was that he didn't like running the electric bill up. Now that I had the place to myself, however, I left it on all the time, turned to high. I hoped he'd have a gigantic bill and go bankrupt.

I made myself a glass of iced coffee and carried it over to the kitchen table. I sat down at the typewriter and looked out the window. The window looked out over an air shaft. A few feet away was the window of another apartment. An old man lived in the apartment and spent his days seated in front of the window reading a newspaper. Once in a while I would catch him looking at me and we'd nod. He'd lived there as long as we'd lived in the apartment, but during all those years I'd never seen him on the street. I began to feel nostalgia for the man and the view out of the window, as though I'd already moved out. I wondered if he'd miss me.

The review didn't take long to write. Even though Meredith had filled me in a little, how long does it take to fake a review of a movie you haven't seen? The answer is, not very long.

I DRESSED in a dark blue linen skirt and a black silk T-shirt for Lincoln Center. The color combination made me feel very Issy Miyake, so I stopped for sushi on the way there. I usually loved going to the film festivals at Lincoln Center, but tonight I would have preferred staying at home and dreaming of vengeance. I knew I was getting very into being a martyr and I didn't know what to do about it. Feeling sorry for myself seemed to be my only interest.

I got there just as the film was starting and took a seat in the last row. The title, *War Zone*, flashed across the screen, and then a soothing, somewhat familiar voice started a voice-over.

The next thing I knew, I woke up, the lights were on and a man was trying to get past me to the aisle. I stood, folding the seat up, to let him pass.

"Excuse me," he said, giving me the kind of disapproving glance that meant he knew I'd slept through the film.

"Was it about Vietnam?" I quickly asked him.

"I'm sorry?"

"The film. Was it about Vietnam?"

"It was about ants," he said, hastening to get by me.

I followed him out into the aisle. "Ants? You mean the insect variety?"

"Yes," he said.

It seemed entirely too coincidental that I had seen two movies about ants in the space of two days. Obviously Woody had once again screwed up my revised schedule. It was going to be hard to complain, though, since I hadn't seen either.

In a way it seemed propitious. Just that morning there had been a line of ants in the kitchen going from the corner of the Formica counter right into the toaster. The problem had been that I hadn't noticed them until after I had eaten my toast. It had made me feel a little sick all day and didn't exactly put me in the mood to write a brilliant review of the film.

Why would anyone want to do a documentary about ants, anyway? What was there to say about them except that they were a nuisance and the more you squashed with your foot, the better the world would be.

Ants didn't constitute a war zone. What constituted a war zone were men and women. And men were the enemy. Nevertheless, I sprayed a little Raid around the kitchen counters before I went to bed. I thought of booby-trapping the apartment before I moved out by spreading enough sugar around in the cracks to guarantee luring every insect in the building into our apartment.

This got me thinking about other tangible forms of revenge. So far my vengeful thoughts had been what might happen in the future. Now I was concentrating on the present. Graffiti on the wall struck me as a good idea. I could buy some cans of spray paint and write pertinent slogans on all the available wall space. Things I would never have the guts to say to Max and Jean in person. Several sprang instantly to mind and I wrote them down so I wouldn't forget. I also thought of melting plastic bottles in the oven and clogging up the toilet and sinks and cutting all the buttons off Max's shirts.

Once I got started there were a million things I could think of. I thought of painting all the windows black and embroidering my name on all the pillowcases and rearranging Max's books so that they were no longer alphabetical and putting a nasty message on his answering machine. I thought of subscribing to the kind of magazines that would embarrass him to receive, of putting a scurrilous bumper sticker on the front door, of sewing the necks of all his T-shirts closed, of buying some mice at the pet store and letting them loose in the apartment. I thought about really evil things like sending an anonymous note to his department head saying that I was a student he had seduced—a male student. Or sending a telegram to his mother saying he had died. Or, and this was the worst I thought of, putting out rat poison in the apartment so that Jean's dog would find it and die. That one even shook me up. I had nothing against her innocent dog and would have sooner put out rat poison for Max.

At six the next morning, still wide awake, I wrote down my two-thousandth idea: putting an ad in the Personals section of the *Voice*, using Max's name and phone number and advertising for a woman.

I wouldn't do any of them, though, and for a very good reason. Max wouldn't hesitate to take me to court for harassment. What's more, he'd win.

No, my revenge had to be more subtle than that. So subtle, in fact, that long afterward Max would still be wondering what hit him.

Chapter Three

Review/FILM
TERROR AT THOMAS JEFFERSON HIGH
SCHOOL, PART SIX
by Ellie Thomas

From the first moment in this film, when Ms. Thornton, the English teacher, (Bette Middling) is seen tastefully adjusting her pantyhose in the teachers' lounge, until the last moment, when Ms. Thornton is found hanging from the net on the basketball court in the school gym, her pantyhose the noose, there is not one scene in this dismally boring movie that could possibly be considered entertaining. If you absolutely have to see a movie and you've seen everything out, with the exception of this, please do yourself a favor and stay home. This latest entry in the Thomas Jefferson High series of low-budget horror flicks is, once again, produced, written, directed and starred in by Mercury Morris. A career move on Mr. Morris's part would seem called for at this point.

Rated R

IT WAS JUST one room, but it had two large windows and a real closet. Down the hall was a bath I would share with two other people and the kitchen was shared by all. I had already been told to put name tags on my food and that the other tenants would prefer not to have red meat stored in the refrigerator.

The woman who owned the lease on the apartment, Philippa Windom, was standing in the doorway watching me for my reaction.

I opened the closet door again for one last look. It even had hooks on the wall in case I didn't want to hang something on a hanger. That appealed to me. Until I married Max, I had never wanted to hang anything on a hanger. "Does the $550 include utilities?" I asked.

"Everything but your telephone," said Philippa.

It was the best thing I'd seen. It was the only place I had seen that I could afford. I hadn't originally thought of a share, but it would do while I waited to see what Max's long-term plans were and also looked around for something else.

"I'll take it," I told Philippa, "If I can move in right away."

"Do you smoke?" asked Philippa.

"No, I don't," I lied. In the not-too-distant past, I wouldn't have lied about that, but times had changed and I had become a member of an oppressed minority. Now, in order to survive, I lied.

"I can smell smoke on your clothes."

"My husband smokes. The smell ought to wash out eventually."

"I usually rent to patients of mine," said the woman, looking undecided over whether to rent to me.

She didn't look like a doctor, not in her Indian cotton clothes, her hands with rings on every finger and her masses of wild, dark hair. I made an educated guess. "Are you a therapist?"

"I'm a healer," said Philippa.

I nodded. "I could really use some healing," I said, willing to try anything in order to get the room. If I didn't get it, how was I going to explain to Max tomorrow that I couldn't move out because I hadn't found a place? He'd probably force me to go to a hotel, and I couldn't afford that. I couldn't even afford the YMCA, which I'd already checked out.

"Are you experiencing a health problem?" asked Philippa.

"Not exactly," I said, "but I'm very depressed over my marriage breaking up."

"Massage often helps depression."

"I'd be willing to give it a try."

"I charge sixty dollars an hour."

I nodded, not committing myself to anything.

"I have another room for rent you might want to take a look at. It has its own bath and I get $750 for it."

"This one will do fine," I said. For two hundred dollars a month I'd stand in line for a bath.

Philippa took what appeared to be a modified flying leap across the room and enfolded me in a big hug. "Welcome," she told me. "I can tell by your aura that you're going to fit in with us beautifully."

"Thanks," I said. It was the most affection anyone had shown me in weeks. It took all of my control not to burst into tears and tell her my troubles.

I HAD SIX THOUSAND five hundred dollars in my savings account. Six thousand had been an inheritance from my grandfather who had died the year before; five hundred I had managed to save during seven years of marriage.

Twelve hundred went for the first and last month's rent on the room, plus a deposit to the telephone company. Another thousand was spent on a futon couch that made into a bed, a bedside table, a table lamp, a secondhand typewriter table and chair and a used IBM Selectric typewriter without the correcting feature. That left me with four thousand three hundred in the bank, which was more money than I had ever had at one time in my life before Grandpa had died.

Other than my clothes, I took very little from the apartment. I took a set of towels that I had recently purchased, an ironing board and iron that Max never used and wouldn't even miss, three stuffed bears that had made the original trip with me from California, and the Pollenex Pure-Air machine that Max had insisted I use to keep my cigarette smoke out of the apartment. Now I was glad I had it. With that, an open window and the artful use of room deodorizers, Philippa need never find out I smoked.

It was Saturday and I was sitting all alone in my room within a vast apartment on West Ninety-seventh Street between Broadway and Amsterdam Avenue. The heat wave still lingered and it was over ninety degrees outside; it was also over ninety in the room. I had been ready to splurge on a window air conditioner but Philippa had said that the wiring in the building wouldn't be able to handle it. I had gone out that morning with the intention of purchasing two fans but found that there had been a run on window fans and all the stores were sold out.

I was tired. I couldn't sleep at night anymore and the only sleep I was getting was a result of the screenings I'd been to all week. Thoughts of revenge kept me awake at night. Thoughts of Max contracting a socially unacceptable disease from Jean and begging me to come back to him. Thoughts of Jean quickly tiring of Max's infantile demand for more and more space. I felt sudden urges in the middle of the night to hear Max's voice. Once I had given in to the urge and dialed his number at three o'clock in the morning. As soon as I heard his voice, I hung up. It hadn't in any way satisfied my urge.

It was a good day to go sit in an air-conditioned movie to cool off except I had already seen seven movies this week and had slept through all seven. At night my dreams of revenge on Max and Jean kept me awake until dawn, but nothing seemed to keep me awake in the screenings anymore. I had found, though, that it was just as easy to write a film review on a movie I'd slept through as it was to write one on a movie I'd seen. Sometimes it was easier as I didn't have any personal feelings about the film to prejudice the review.

I got out my address book to call some of my friends to see if anyone was in the city for the weekend. Maybe one of them with an air-conditioned apartment would invite me over. The first one I called had a message on her machine saying she was at her summer place in the Hamptons. The second and third left messages that they were taking advantage of the hot weekend to get away to their weekend homes in the country.

I had always wanted to have a place to get away to on the weekends. Max, who had grown up in the city, never saw the need for one. The one time I had talked him into spending a weekend at a country inn in Vermont, he had become almost psychotic after one night of silence and we had returned to the city the next day.

I had my address book open to the S's when I noticed Alicia Quattro Stern's name. I hadn't seen Alicia in years. Even so, I knew Alicia and Richard would be at the same address because when you had an apartment as good as theirs you didn't move. Richard had inherited the apartment from his parents when they had retired to Florida. I really envied born New Yorkers who inherited apartments. True, Max might inherit his mother's apartment some day, but neither of us had any desire to live in a tiny, fifth-floor walk-up in Coney Island.

I was glad I had come across Alicia's name because she lived only a few blocks away on Riverside Drive in the eighties. We were neighbors again and maybe we could repair our friendship. I could use a friend of my own. Just about everyone else in my phone book whom I considered a friend was really just the wife of one of Max's friends. They might not even want to see me anymore now that Max and I had split up.

I was suddenly remembering Alicia and recalling how close we once had been. I didn't even care if she invited me over to her air-conditioned apartment, I just wanted to talk to her. How could we have ever lost touch the way we had?

I punched out Alicia's number. I had meant to spend a little time chatting with her, after all, we hadn't spoken in years, but the second Alicia picked up and said, "Hello," I found myself blurting out, "This is Ellie. Max and I split up."

There were a couple of seconds of silence, no doubt while Alicia tried to place me, and then Alicia said, "Great. It's about time."

I belatedly remembered why we hadn't spoken in years. It was because Alicia and Richard didn't like Max.

"I just moved into a share, in a building not far from you," I said. "I was thinking maybe—"

"Welcome to the Upper Westside."

"Thank you."

"So you finally left him. Good for you. What took you seven years, Ellie?"

"Well, I didn't exactly leave him."

"Max dumped *you*?"

"I'm afraid so."

"The idiot," said Alicia, the scorn in her voice making me smile.

"What've you been doing, Alicia?"

"Are you free tonight?"

"I'm free all weekend," I said.

"Perfect. We're having a party tonight."

"I don't know if I'm ready for a party. I thought I'd take things a little slow at first. Maybe we could have lunch next week."

"You're ready. After being married to Max for seven years, you're more than ready."

"I don't know," I said, wanting her to talk me into it. She had always been an expert at talking me into things.

"Come on, it's going to be mostly film and theater people; they'll be thrilled to meet a reviewer. I always read your reviews, you know. I usually get a good laugh out of them. Although lately..."

"I haven't really been into them lately."

"I could tell. Well, now I know the reason."

"You still doing editing, Alicia?"

"Did you hear?"

"Hear what?"

"I finally got accepted into the union. If I were a man I would've gotten in years ago, of course. I finally got to edit a feature film."

"It's not out yet, is it?" I asked.

"No, I'm still editing it. And when it does come out, Ellie, I expect—never mind, forget I said that. I've got to remember I can't talk that way to reviewers anymore.

Although you know something, Ellie? Now that I'm finally legit, I've kind of lost interest in editing. It's not really all that fulfilling.''

"Is it a horror film?"

"Don't be ridiculous."

"Then I wouldn't be reviewing it, anyway. I'd really like to hear all about it, Alicia."

"Then you definitely have to come to the party."

I thought of going to a party and having to meet new people. Having to talk to men. It had been a long time since I had gone to a party without Max. Still, a party sounded better than staying home alone in my hot room all weekend. Even if I did have to hear about how Alicia finally made it and wasn't finding it fulfilling, while I was still reviewing movies for the same lousy paper I had started with.

"I'd love to come," I told her.

I WAS LATE to the party because one of the men I shared the bathroom with had decided that Saturday night was a good time to take a bath, and he had hogged the bathroom for over an hour and a half. When he finally emerged, he was no more than a shadowy figure in the hall, and I passed him without a word.

The bathroom looked and felt like a steam room and had no window to let the steam out. I took a cold shower and afterward I checked out the medicine cabinet. It was filled with mostly male-type things: shaving cream, disposable razors, after-shave, Preparation H. There was also a can of spray intended for jock itch. Judging by the wet towels on the floor, the empty toilet paper holder and the contents of the medicine cabinet, both people I shared the bathroom with appeared to be male.

I carried my own towel back to my room to let it dry. I didn't mind sharing the shower, but I wasn't about to share my towel. Particularly not with someone with jock itch.

A Saturday-night party in the summer meant shorts, and I found a clean pair of tan shorts and a dark green T-shirt that was only slightly wrinkled. I thought of ironing it but it was just too hot to plug in the steam iron. I managed the semblance of a French braid with my damp hair and briefly considered makeup. It didn't seem worthwhile bothering, though, since I'd no doubt sweat it off while walking to the party.

I was sitting on the couch tying my sneakers when there was a knock at the door. I threw my cigarette out the window, then yelled, "Come on in." The door opened and Philippa looked in.

"All settled?" she asked, looking around the room.

"Everything's great," I said, prone to exaggeration both in reviews and in life.

"I'm giving a healing demonstration in the living room in fifteen minutes, if you're interested. It'd give you a chance to meet some of the others."

"Thanks," I said, "but I'm going to a party."

"Enjoy yourself," said Philippa, "that sounds like a lot more fun."

I wasn't so sure. In fact with a little persuasion, I might have opted to stay home.

The last thing I did before leaving my room was to remove my wedding band.

I STOOD amongst a group of people, all of them talking about someone I didn't know, all of them acting hyper and in a party mode, all of them ignoring me. I kept a half smile on my face and tried to pretend I was enjoying the conversation. I had already had a glass of red wine with ice in it, was on my second, and neither one was helping. I felt out of place and out of it; I guessed I'd been married too long. When I went to parties with Max, I had something to do. Max always expounded on his film theories and I always was part of his listening audience. I felt naked without my wedding ring and Max by my side for protection. Feeling naked made me wonder where Max was. He was probably in our air-conditioned apartment in our large comfortable bed...with Jean. Naked. I got so angry at the thought I dropped my smile.

Alicia had been friendly when I arrived, but the party was now wall-to-wall people extending through the seven rooms, out into the hall, up the stairs and out onto the roof. I noticed that no one inside the apartment was smoking and decided that the smokers were probably congregated on top of the building.

I returned the smile to my face and was backing out of the group and preparing to maneuver my way through the crowd to the stairs, when Richard, Alicia's husband, blocked my way.

"Elinor!" he exclaimed. "It *is* you. Alicia didn't mention you were coming."

"Alicia invited me," I said.

"I'm not questioning your right to be here, I'm just expressing my surprise. Where's Max?"

"Alicia didn't mention that, either?"

"Not you and Max," said Richard, in such a way that I knew Alicia had mentioned it.

Maybe Alicia and Richard hadn't liked Max, but Max and I hadn't liked Richard, either. Richard, unlike most of our friends, wasn't involved in film. Richard was involved in the theater and never let us forget it. Richard considered anyone involved in film to be greedy opportunists who had sold out to commercialism. Times had changed, though, and Richard had became somewhat commercial himself. He still directed occasionally. Off Broadway, but I had also heard he was directing soaps for good money.

A young man—in fact a very young man, and very good-looking—came up to Richard, saying, "Great party, Rich." I had a feeling that the man was saying it more to me than to Richard, only that didn't make any sense. It wasn't likely he was interested in me. It had been some time since young, good-looking men looked me over on the street or tried to pick me up on the subway.

Richard looked around. "Glad you could make it, Scott. Do you know Ellie Thomas? She's a film critic. Ellie, this is Scott Parker. You've probably seen him on TV."

Scott seemed to be waiting for some sign of recognition from me. Well, he wasn't going to get it because Max had never allowed a television set in our home. Not even to hook up a VCR to in order to watch movies. Half the celebrities on the cover of *People* I didn't even recognize.

Richard wandered off, and I expected Scott to do the same, but instead he moved in closer to me. He was tall and tan and had chiseled features and blond curls that hung artfully over his forehead. He was dressed in tennis whites. He looked like every young girl's dream, but, unfortunately, he also looked very much like my younger brother, Pete. He was smiling at me and his eyes were dancing and he was obviously waiting for me to say something. I briefly wondered whether I had reached that point in my life where I qualified as an "interesting older woman." If that's what he was expecting, I was sure I was going to flub the "interesting" part.

I didn't want to flunk party going my first time out as a single, so I asked him, "Are you from the Coast?" figuring he couldn't have gotten that tan so early in the summer in New York.

"No. Our series is shot in New York."

"Oh," I said.

"What network do you review for?" he asked.

"I review for a newspaper."

"The *Times*?"

"No, *Views and Reviews*."

"Oh. I never read that. I'll have to get it and check out your reviews."

"Don't bother. I review the horror films."

"I love horror films," said Scott, his smile growing broader, if possible. "Have you seen the new Thomas Jefferson High School one? It's a real classic."

"I reviewed it," I said, hoping he wouldn't want to discuss it in depth.

"It was great. I saw it last night and walked out of the theater stunned."

I was getting nervous. What if he asked me to the movies? He was so young and so beautiful and I wasn't up to it. Maybe we were the only ones there without dates. How did I ever let Alicia talk me into this?

I looked around for a means of escape. I noticed several young women watching me in envy. Young women had never watched me in envy when I had been at parties with Max, unless they were his students, so it was a new experience. I looked back at Scott, trying to see what they saw. Whatever it was, it wasn't there for me.

Scott was still going on about the movie, and I looked toward the door to the hallway, wondering if I could just walk off in the middle of his monologue. I saw an older man, tired looking, maybe forty-five, watching me. He looked familiar but I couldn't put a name to him. He was wearing a white T-shirt with some small, black writing across the chest. When I caught his eye, he gave what looked like a smile of commiseration. I didn't smile back. He looked as though he wouldn't mind having a young blonde talking to him, so I didn't know what he was commiserating with me about.

I turned back to Scott and interrupted him mid-sentence. "Actually, I was looking for the bathroom," I said to him. Things had reached the point where it was more socially acceptable to be looking for the bathroom than to be going up to the roof for a smoke.

"Oh, sure," said Scott, "it's down the hall to your right. I'll meet you back here."

"I thought I'd go up to the roof for some air."

"It's hot up there," said Scott.

"I don't mind. I feel like some air."

"Whatever you say," said Scott. "I'll see you up there, then." He was young *and* persistent. He had to be playing some sort of game with me for the benefit of those younger admirers of his.

I went to the bathroom and stood looking at myself in the mirror for the required amount of time. I thought maybe there was some change in me that I hadn't noticed in the fogged-up mirror in my bathroom. However, I looked the way I always looked; what's more, I looked my age. So why was the blond Adonis coming on to me? What did I suddenly have that I hadn't had for the past thirty-five years?

And why the hell wasn't Max there to scare him off?

SEVERAL GROUPS of people stood around on the roof pretending to enjoy the sight of Manhattan lit up below them, but actually trying to get their nicotine levels up enough to return to the party downstairs.

I was on my third glass of wine and hoping this one worked. So far all it was doing was making me warm. I lit a cigarette and took a deep drag, then heard a familiar whisper at my side.

"I'm glad to see you awake," he said, and I immediately recognized the voice from the screening room.

I turned too fast and my red wine ended up soaking the front of his white T-shirt. What I had previously thought was small writing now turned out to be little black ants marching across his chest.

"Oh, God, I'm sorry," I said, knowing red wine didn't wash out of anything.

"I'm getting used to it," he said, sounding amused.

"I don't even have anything to wipe it up with."

"At least it felt better than the hot coffee."

I thought it kind of rude to bring that up, so I countered with, "I can't believe you liked that movie well enough to buy a T-shirt advertising it."

This, I could see, ticked him off, but he didn't get to reply because Scott showed up then and immediately yelled at me, "Hey, those are going to kill you, you know."

I choked on the smoke.

"Come on, don't you care about your health?"

"I don't need a lecture, Scott."

"If you don't care about your health, then think about the lines it's giving you. You really age fast from smoking."

I could've killed him. I saw the man wearing the ants backing off. He probably figured I got my comeuppance without his help.

Age fast, indeed! What was going to age me fast was this kid who wouldn't see thirty for some time. I heard a deep rumble of laughter and turned in time to see that it came from the ant man. He was also smoking. Maybe he wasn't as old as I thought; maybe he'd just aged from smoking. Maybe Scott was really a man of fifty but had retained his boyish good looks because he'd never lit a cigarette.

Maybe I should go home and watch the healing demonstration.

"You want to go get some dinner?" Scott was asking me.

"I don't quite see the attraction," I said, fully aware that I was now playing to an audience.

"I'm hungry, that's all," said Scott.

"I mean the attraction for me. How old are you?"

"Twenty-eight. Why?"

"I'm thirty-five."

"No problem. I like older women."

"Why?"

"Because they have their act together."

I didn't feel I had my act together. A month ago I thought I did, but now I wasn't even sure what my act was. Certainly having to share an apartment with a bunch of roommates at thirty-five wasn't my idea of having my act together. Nor was a husband who left me for my best friend.

"What do you say? You want to get something to eat?"

"I believe Alicia has food downstairs."

"You want to go down and get some?"

I dropped my cigarette and ground it out on the roof. He was obviously not going to be easy to get rid of. I'd get some food, enjoy the air-conditioning for a little longer, and then go home. Maybe tonight would be the night I'd be able to sleep.

ALICIA DREW ME ASIDE. She was still small and dark, but her long hair had been cut to shoulder length and parted on the side so that it fell across her face whenever she moved. She wore much less eye makeup than she had worn in college and, as a result, looked younger and more innocent. "I see you've become acquainted with Scott," she said. Her voice was still husky with the ironic tone to it that she had perfected when we were still in school. "He's a cutie, isn't he?"

"You find him attractive?" I asked her.

"Are you kidding? Several million women find him attractive. I'm no exception."

"If I'd known that, I would've fixed you up with my brother years ago."

"You have a brother who looks like that?"

"Similar."

"And I never got to meet him?"

"You wouldn't have been interested. He was in high school at the time."

"So what's happening, has he asked you out yet?"

"Alicia, I find him very young and not at all appealing."

"Would it kill you for once, Ellie, to go for a guy with looks? It's not like you're ugly. It's not like you're going to walk into a room with him and everyone's going to think he's prettier than you are."

"Tell me another one."

"He just seems like a nice change of pace."

"I thought you went for guys with intellect."

"That was in college. After being married for six years to a guy with intellect, I think I'm ready for a change."

"Are you and Richard having problems?"

"No. Not really. It's just that a guy who looked good and didn't talk all the time might be a novelty. For either one of us."

"Scott talks."

"Yes, but he doesn't say anything profound."

I said, "I don't like actors."

"What kind of a generalization is that? How many actors have you dated in your life?"

"None."

"I rest my case."

"How could you possibly get serious about an actor?"

"Ellie, you've been separated how long, a week?"

I nodded.

"And you're already looking to get serious?"

"I'm not looking for anything."

"That's what I mean. So you go out with Scott, you have a good time. I hear he's got a summer place on Fire Island and a loft in Soho to die for."

I thought of spending weekends out of the city all summer. Maybe the age difference really wasn't important. I saw the older, wine-stained man heading out the front door and asked Alicia, "Who's that man leaving? The one in the jeans with holes in them."

Alicia looked around. "You mean Sam? You know Sam, don't you?"

"If I knew him, I wouldn't ask."

"You must know him."

"Look, it's not important."

"Sam Wiley. You reviewed one of his films this week."

Two and two finally added up and the total came crashing down on my head. "Wait a minute. The one about the ants?"

She nodded. "You hated it."

It wasn't that I hated it. I just couldn't imagine that anyone would be interested in a film about ants.

She finished me off with, "All the other reviewers loved it."

I said, "I hope he doesn't know who I am."

"He knows," said Alicia. "He asked me."

"Was he upset about the review?"

"He was probably confused, just as I was. You always loved his films before. You called him 'the most innovative documentary filmmaker working today."

"*I* said that?"

"You said that when you reviewed his cockroach movie."

"Wait a minute. The one where he compared cockroaches to New Yorkers?"

"Right."

"I *loved* that."

"I know you did, El. That's what I'm telling you."

"I think he's great."

"Then I'm sure you were fair in your review. Anyway, ants just aren't as interesting as cockroaches."

"It's not that cockroaches are so interesting; it's him. The way he thinks. He has a quirky way of looking at things that I really find amusing."

"I imagine Scott can be amusing at times."

"I spilled wine all over him," I said, to say nothing of hot coffee.

"Scott?"

"No, Sam Wiley." He was here and I hadn't even gotten to know him. I couldn't believe it. I'd always wanted to meet him. I'd have given anything to have made one of his films.

Alicia shook her head. "I should've known you'd go for Sam."

"I don't *go* for him, Alicia. I go for his films."

"Do yourself a favor and change types, El."

"What are you talking about?"

"The fact that he's practically a clone for Max. Same dark curly hair, same beard, same horn-rimmed glasses, same intellect—everything, in fact, but the same age. Wouldn't you like a change?"

"I just would have liked to talk to him about his films, that's all."

"Plus, he's never in town long enough to even get to know. Look at Scott over there—he can't take his eyes off you. Do yourself a favor and have some fun this summer. Think of weekends on Fire Island."

"What I really want to do, Alicia, is hear about your movie."

"Not now, sweetie, I've got to mingle. Let's have lunch this week and I'll tell you all about it."

The weekends on Fire Island didn't change my mind about Scott, nor did Alicia's other persuasions. What really made me change my mind was the thought of running into Max and Jean on the street, which was bound to happen sooner or later, and having them see me with a young, good-looking, famous guy. I formed a picture of Max dying of jealousy and Jean lusting for Scott. It would be a very satisfying form of revenge.

And so, when Alicia took off into the crowd and Scott came up to me and asked me if I wanted to take a walk, I told him yes. I thought he might be more interesting away from the party, he couldn't possibly object to my smoking on the street, and an added benefit would be that the exercise might help me go to sleep.

I was wrong on all counts.

Scott's idea of a walk was strolling down Columbus Avenue and looking in the windows of all the men's shops. My idea of a walk was heading into Central Park, where I thought it might be cooler. We compromised by heading down Columbus Avenue as far as Seventy-second Street and then heading a few yards into the park. At the first bench, he decided we should take a rest.

I lit up.

He started on a lecture about smoking. It was not only bad for my health and sure to prematurely age me, but it was also a filthy, antisocial habit.

I felt like saying that lecturing was also a filthy, anti-social habit, but demurred. Instead I put out my cigarette. "Tell me about your series, Scott," I said, and then promptly fell asleep on the bench. I don't know how long Scott talked on before he noticed it, but I felt rather refreshed when he shook me awake.

"I'll walk you home," he said.

I felt like a dud.

Chapter Four

Review/FILM
KEN KILLS
by Ellie Thomas

For those of us who played with Barbie and Ken dolls as children, the idea of a movie about a Ken doll imbued with an evil spirit is intriguing. In *Ken Kills*, however, we are intrigued for about two minutes. After that we are forced to wonder how an entire family could be terrorized by a ten-inch skinny doll that any member of the family, including the five-year-old (played unconvincingly by Tyne Daily) could have demolished by placing a foot over the doll and stepping down hard. A good performance by Oprah Wimpy as the mother serves to make the rest of the movie look amateurish by comparison. If you're willing to pay seven dollars to see this disaster, I've got a bridge over to Brooklyn I'd like to interest you in buying.

Rated X

I MET ALICIA for lunch in Soho. Alicia looked cool and unwrinkled in knee-length brown linen shorts and a cream silk shirt. I figured she had to have stepped right out of her air-conditioned apartment and into an air-conditioned taxi. In the time it took me to get out of a cold shower in the morning and into my clothes, I was already sweating.

The Prince Street Restaurant wasn't known for its food, but the place was cool and uncrowded and we got a table to ourselves at the window.

Alicia looked at me and shook her head. "Why haven't we been doing this for years, El? What happened to us?"

"We got married."

"Sure, but we still could've met for lunch."

The waiter brought menus and without even looking we both ordered chef salads and ice tea.

"You look good," I told her. "Younger than you looked in college."

"Come on."

"No, you do. I like your hair."

Alicia's hand went up to sweep her hair back off her face. "You've hardly changed. You look a little tired, though."

"A little?" I felt the bags under my eyes with my fingertips. Yes, they were still there.

"Prescriptives has some gel out; you put it under your eyes in the morning and the bags disappear."

"I'd settle for a little sleep," I told her. I asked her about the feature film she was editing, wanting to change the subject. My lack of sleep was not fit conversation for the lunch table.

"You want to hear something ironic, El? All these years I've been trying to get in the union, and now that I'm in, I'm bored with editing."

"I thought you loved to edit."

"I did. For the first few years. I don't know, the challenge seems to be gone. All I get out of it these days is a headache. Anyway, editing someone else's work just isn't creatively satisfying."

The salads arrived and we settled in to eat.

"I'm bored with reviewing bad movies, too," I said.

"You wouldn't know it to read them."

"Thanks."

"Really. They're quite funny."

"Trying to make the reviews funny is the only thing that keeps me amused."

"Why don't you try to get with another paper? You're really popular; I'm sure one of the dailies would jump at the chance to get you."

"If they want me, all they have to do is call. Anyway, I think I'd like a change."

"To what?"

"I have no idea."

"It always sounded ideal to me," said Alicia.

"Would you really want to see a movie every day of the week?"

"Well, no," said Alicia, "but then I can barely manage a half hour of news on the TV at night."

"Max wouldn't allow a TV in the apartment."

"I wouldn't, either, until Richard started directing for TV and insisted on it."

"It couldn't be any worse than watching horror films."

Alicia lowered her voice a little and said, "You know what I've been doing lately?"

She made it sound mysterious, as though she were having an affair. "What?" I asked her.

"Writing little stories."

"Short stories?"

"Not exactly. More like little vignettes of my life. I don't know where they come from and I don't know what to do with them, but I keep writing them."

"I think that's great. Maybe you'll end up an author."

Alicia shook her head. "I don't think so. I wouldn't want to do that all the time. I like working around other people, not being locked up in a room by myself."

I didn't think I'd mind being locked up in a room by myself as long as that room was air-conditioned.

The waiter stopped by to see if we wanted any dessert. Alicia looked at me and I grinned. "What the hell," said Alicia, "we might as well hear them."

We decided on raspberries and cream, which we felt we deserved after the salads.

"What exactly happened between you and Max?" asked Alicia.

"You don't want to hear."

"You know that's not true, El. I'm dying to hear."

"I caught him and the woman I thought was my best friend."

"Your *best friend*?"

"We weren't all that close, not the way you and I used to be, but she lived in the building and I saw a lot of her."

"I guess you both saw a lot of her. Sorry, I couldn't help it."

"No, I'm sure you're right."

"Where'd you catch them?"

"It was like some French farce. The projector broke down during the screening, so I arrived home early, and the two of them were stark naked in the living room."

Alicia's eyes widened. "Doing it?"

I shook my head. "Not really. It looked more like fun and games. Chasing each other around, that sort of thing."

"My God, how embarrassing!"

"It's crazy. What went through my mind at the time was why Max would prefer a woman with cellulite on her thighs and great, drooping breasts. She wasn't a pretty sight."

Alicia started to chuckle. "What did you do?"

"What *could* I do? I walked back out and left them to it."

"I'm surprised. Max doesn't seem the type to have an affair."

"They're all the type."

"I suppose." Her eyes began to gleam. "I caught Richard at something once, but it wasn't quite that flagrant."

There was a long pause and I finally said, "Am I going to hear about it?"

"I suppose. It was at a party. I walked into the bedroom to get something out of my handbag and Richard was kissing one of the young actresses on the show he was directing."

"And you walked out and ignored it."

"No way," said Alicia. "I took off my wedding ring and handed it to her, reminded Richard it was time to take his herpes medication, and then wished them both luck before walking out."

"Does Richard have herpes?"

"He better not," said Alicia, "but you can bet the news traveled around the set within twenty-four hours. I don't think any young actresses will be eager to fool around with him anymore."

We paid the check and walked over to West Broadway. We stopped in Henry Lehr and admired the clothes, then crossed Houston and headed into the Village.

"So, have you met any men?" asked Alicia.

"Why should I want to meet any men? I would think after seven years of marriage I deserve a rest."

"In the winter maybe, but I always think it's nice to have a little romance in the summer."

"Scott keeps calling me."

"So go out with him."

"I still feel married."

"So pretend you're sneaking around on Max. It might be fun."

"I'm so intent on getting revenge on Max, I can't get interested in anything else. I can't even sleep anymore, Alicia. I stay awake all night trying to think up ways to get even with him."

"Then get your revenge. Once you do, you'll probably be able to sleep."

"I have to find the perfect way."

"The perfect way," said Alicia, "is always another man. And Scott should be the perfect candidate. I know Richard would be livid if I took up with a younger, better-looking man."

I nodded. "I've thought of that. Of running into them when I'm with Scott. But that could take months and I don't think I could stand Scott for months. Look at us, all these years in the same city and we've never run into each other."

"But you must know Max's schedule. It shouldn't be so hard to just happen to run into him."

"I guess I could arrange it."

"Do it. And, El—be sure and let me know how it turns out."

We hugged on the street corner, then went our separate ways.

I SAT AT THE SMALL, round table at one of the trendy sidewalk cafés on Columbus Avenue and wished I'd stayed home. The food—which was supposed to be Mexican but was like nothing I'd ever tasted—was making me sick, the heat was oppressive, and Scott was boring.

My only excuse for being there was that I wasn't used to being pursued. Scott had called me at least twice a day since the party, asking me to go out. I couldn't figure out what his problem was. There were younger women around, whom I felt sure would be thrilled to go out with him. There were better looking women around. There was nothing as a film critic that I could do for him since he didn't appear in movies. It was unlikely he went for my intellect since he seldom gave me a chance to speak. I came to the conclusion that the only attraction was that he couldn't stand rejection and I was probably giving him a harder time than any of the women he had dated.

I also went because I wanted to get out of my neighborhood. I had come out of my building that morning to a shocking sight. Strung across my street was a large, yellow banner. At first I thought my block was going to hold a street fair. Then I read the large black letters on the banner: Police are Watching This Crack Block. I saw a man come out of a building across the street and also notice the banner. He looked over at me and then we both quickly avoided the other's eyes. I was wondering if he was a crack dealer; I was sure he was wondering the same thing about me. It was enough to instill guilt in the most innocent of people.

So when Scott called me at the office after I left Alicia, I finally agreed to have dinner with him. I no longer felt like eating my meals at the coffee shop on my block, and I was also hoping to get him down to the Village where we might run into Max and Jean. Jean always walked around Washington Square Park ten times after dinner for exercise, and I thought there was a chance Max might be joining her in that walk. Scott and I could just be happening to walk by the park at that time and just happen to run into them.

Scott, however, had refused to go to the village. He said no one went to the Village anymore. He said it was always filled with tourists in the summer and tourists always besieged him for autographs. I thought that would be perfect. Max would die if I were with someone who was being besieged for autographs.

Scott, however, was adamant. He promised me we'd go to the Village another time when he was wearing his dark glasses and a wig. I didn't point out to him that if he was going to be in a disguise, he could forget going out with me.

So there we were, eating pseudo-Mexican food, while Scott talked at great length about his health club. That was all right. Everyone I knew spoke at great length of their health clubs. He bragged to me that his tan was from tanning machines, even though he had a house at the beach. He confessed that he had porcelain caps, even pointing them out to me on his teeth. He was now telling me about the benefits of Retin-A and how I might think about trying it in order to reduce the lines around my eyes. I had always known I wouldn't like dating an actor and he was proving me right.

I was beginning to see what he saw in me. I was an audience. If he dated another actor, he'd have to share his performance time. I found that I was tired of being an audience for men. I felt like discussing social problems, not the lines around my eyes.

Scott was still talking when the waiter asked if we wanted dessert. The waiter was also an actor, trying to act cool about serving Scott but not succeeding. He spent some time with Scott over the dessert menu, presonally recommending or rejecting all of the available choices. Scott finally decided on chocolate mousse cheesecake and I declined. As soon as he finished his dessert, I was going to tell him I wanted to go home. Then I'd sneak out to Häagen-Dazs and buy my own dessert.

Scott was talking about how tiresome it was, being recognized wherever he went, but I noticed that all the while he was talking about it, he was also catching the eye of various of his fans and smiling broadly at them. He had been the center of attention ever since we sat down.

I looked around and noted how many of the women were watching Scott. Maybe that's why he asked me out. Maybe he liked to be seen with someone no one ever noticed so that none of the attention was deflected from him. It was then I saw Sam Wiley. He was easy to notice because he was the only one at the sidewalk café who was looking at me rather than at Scott.

I began to wonder why he was looking at me. Could he be so incensed by the review I gave his ant movie that he wanted to berate me? Possibly. Had he fallen in love with my stunning good looks at the party? Not likely. Was he actually interested in Scott and looking to me as a way of meeting him? Could be. I should be the one looking at him, not the other way around, since I was a great fan of his.

Forgetting we hadn't even been introduced, I found myself smiling at him. He not only returned the smile, he got up from his table and approached ours. He was wearing his torn jeans again and a new T-shirt with a picture of an insect on it. It was enlarged, but I figured it was an ant. All the other men at the sidewalk café were wearing shorts and I wondered whether Sam Wiley was hiding lousy legs or whether he had some sentimental attachment to those jeans.

Without even being invited, he sat down with us, saying, "Wasn't that a great party at Alicia and Richard's Saturday night?" I knew that was for Scott's benefit.

Up close I didn't think he and Max looked much alike. For one thing Sam looked kinder, but maybe it was just that he had a lot of laugh lines. Max didn't have any. But Sam had touches of gray in his beard whereas Max's highlights were red. Max also wouldn't be caught dead in jeans with holes in them or without his silk scarf thrown around his neck. Max was pretentious, but his only saving grace was that he knew he was pretentious.

I smiled at Sam. "I'm Ellie," I said, holding out my hand, "and this is Scott."

Scott said, "Hi," then waited to be recognized. Sam introduced himself to me and ignored Scott.

"I've got a bone to pick with you," Sam said to me, while Scott started busying himself with his dessert.

"What's that?" I asked, hoping it wasn't about what I thought it was about.

"That review you wrote of my entry in the film festival. I know we're not supposed to complain to reviewers, but I didn't know reviewers were supposed to sleep through films."

"I call them as I see them," I said, wishing now I'd never smiled at him across the café. I admired his guts, though, in confronting a critic head-on.

"I spend six months of my life shooting down on the Amazon, another two months editing, and you demolish it in two paragraphs." His tone was genial, but that didn't fool me. He was angry about my review.

"What movie was that?" asked Scott, who had suddenly started to show an interest when movies were mentioned. "I probably saw it."

"It was a documentary about ants," I told him. Scott went back to eating his dessert. Anyone making documentaries wasn't likely to star him in his next one.

"That sounds fascinating," I said, "living on the Amazon for six months." Actually it sounded dreadful. I was sure the jungle wasn't air-conditioned. I was also sure it was infested with insects. Ones even larger and more frightening than ants.

"It *was* fascinating. I'm in town arranging funding at the moment so I can go back down there and make another"

"Another one on ants?"

"Why would I make another on ants? How many movies do you think people want to see about ants?"

I hadn't wanted to see the first one.

Sam started to talk about the hundreds of different species of butterflies on the Amazon, and I stopped listening. Did all men require an audience? This wasn't any more interesting than listening to Scott discuss Retin-A. I didn't know why I had been pleased to see him join us. The only difference between the two was that one was an older man wanting to talk about himself and the other was a younger man wanting to do the same thing. Maybe I wanted to talk about myself; did they ever think of that?

Sam was still talking about butterflies, comparing them to Southern Californians, when Scott called the waiter over for the check. I could tell that Scott was somewhat annoyed at having lost his audience. I had a feeling he was going to excuse himself and tell me to stay on if I wanted. I wondered if I should beat him to it and excuse myself first. Sitting out here on Columbus Avenue wasn't any better than sitting in my room, with the exception that I was allowed to smoke here. I hadn't, though, because I didn't want to hear any more dreadful warnings from Scott.

Sure enough, after Scott paid the bill, he turned to me and said, "I've got to be up early."

"I think I'll just stay and have a cigarette," I said, already reaching into my bag for a pack.

"I'll call you then," said Scott.

"Let me pay for my half of the bill," I said.

"You can get the check next time."

Great. Now I felt obligated to go out with him again. Sam's eyes looked ambiguous as Scott walked off. I lit my cigarette and ignored him.

"I feel used," said Sam.

"You do?"

"You used me to get rid of him, didn't you?"

"Yes," I admitted. "Do you mind?"

"I could have been anyone."

"That's true."

Sam shrugged. "Well, what the hell, it's not as though we know each other. And you did look as though you were dying of boredom. I figure I've done my good deed for the day."

"I heard about his beauty routine," I told him.

"He's a good-looking guy."

"Yes."

"And from me you heard about butterflies. Probably not much of an improvement, from your perspective."

"I'm not very good company these days."

He gave me a serious look, tapping his lips with his finger. "How long's it been?"

"How long has what been?"

"Since you split up?"

"Did Alicia tell you that?"

"She didn't have to tell me; I know the signs. I've been divorced five years."

"It's only been ten days," I said.

"Oh, well—it takes at least a year just to get human again."

Not exactly what I wanted to hear. "That long?"

"It took me more like eighteen months."

I contemplated eighteen months of not being able to sleep at night and shuddered. "Were you able to sleep at night?"

"Not too well, and only if I'd had several drinks."

I decided that I'd rather be an insomniac than a drunk. He was being so nice, though, that I said, "I'm sorry."

"No need; I'm all over it."

"I mean about the movie review. You see, I haven't been able to sleep at night, so I've been falling asleep in the screenings. It wasn't just yours."

A slow smile spread across his face, making him look younger. Still old, but not as old as I'd thought. "I'm relieved to hear it wasn't just mine."

"I can't promise I would've liked it any better if I'd been awake."

"You would've. You liked all my others. In fact you always seemed to understand what I was trying to do."

"The cockroach one was my favorite."

"I cut out your review and framed it."

"My review?"

"It's hanging in my mother's kitchen."

"It's not that I like cockroaches, but I like the narratives you do. They're funny."

"The only way to make cockroaches palatable to the public is to make them funny. Most of the reviewers found my latest one funny."

"I really wish I'd stayed awake now."

"It's not too late. I can arrange a special screening for you."

"But I've already reviewed it."

"The hell with the review. I just want to get your opinion on it. Anyway, the *Times* gave me a great review."

"And they're the ones who count."

"You said it. I didn't. How about if I set it up for tomorrow night? You free?"

"Tomorrow night's fine. I'd really like to see it." I dropped my cigarette on the sidewalk and stepped on it. At the prices they charged, they could at least provide ashtrays. I found it was relaxing to be with someone who wasn't always counting how many cigarettes I smoked. Max had once kept a chart on the kitchen wall. I set fire to it one day with my cigarette lighter and he never tried that again.

I said, "I'd love to be able to make films like that."

"You mean you have aspirations beyond critiquing?"

"I used to."

"What happened to them?"

"The usual."

"What usual?"

I shrugged. "I got married."

"That's no excuse."

"My husband seemed more talented, so I guess I just deferred to him."

"What films has he made?"

"He hasn't made any, other than the ones he made as a student. He teaches cinematography at NYU."

Sam lit a cigarette and offered me one. The waiter immediately ran over and told us we were sitting in a No Smoking section.

"Outdoors?" I asked him. "How can we be bothering anyone outdoors?"

"It's the law," said the waiter.

"If they can stand the exhaust from the cars..." I started to argue, but Sam got up, saying, "Let's take a walk."

He started to head uptown, but I got him turned around and headed in the direction of Häagen Dazs. There was a long line out the door and onto the sidewalk. When they finally took our order, I ordered vanilla.

"Hold it!" Sam said to the sales clerk. "Come on, Ellie, you can't really want vanilla. Nobody likes vanilla."

"I always order vanilla."

"I figured you for a more interesting choice than that."

"I'm sloppy."

"You're sloppy?"

"I prefer chocolate, but I always spill on myself and vanilla doesn't leave a stain." And Max always got upset when I walked around with chocolate all over my clothes. "Anyway, at the rate things have been going, it would probably be you I'd spill it on, and I'd hate to ruin another one of your T-shirts."

"If you spill, I'll buy you a new T-shirt," he said, ordering us both chocolate chocolate chip. I felt a little daring being with a man who ordered chocolate chocolate chip. Max always ordered peach. "And if you spill on mine," he added, "you can wash it for me."

We started walking uptown. It was so hot out that the ice cream melted immediately, running down the sides of the cone faster than I could lick it up. Brown spots dotted my T-shirt before we had walked a block. I wondered what kind of T-shirt he'd buy for me or whether I'd end up with one with ants on it to promote his film.

"Do you live around here?" I asked him.

"A friend has been letting me use his apartment on Eighty-sixth Street while he's away. He's coming back Friday, though, and I've got to find a place. You don't happen to know of any sublets around here, do you?"

"That's what I was looking for."

"Did you find one?"

"All I found was a room. This woman has this huge apartment and she rents out rooms."

"Does she have any more for rent?"

"There's one with its own bath for $750 that's still available."

"You know what you can get on the Amazon for $750 a month?"

"Probably your own tribe," I said.

"Just about."

"Seven-fifty's not bad these days and you don't have to put down two months' rent in advance."

"Is it air-conditioned?"

"No."

"Furnished?"

"No."

"Will you put in a good word for me?"

"How's your health?" I asked him.

"I get flare-ups of malaria once in a while."

"Great," I said. "The woman who owns the apartment is a healer. Tell her you have a medical problem and she'll be thrilled to rent to you. She might even give you a discount. Just don't tell her you smoke."

"What happened?" Sam asked. "I was only out of the country for a few months and when I get back I can't smoke anywhere."

I was just about to go into my political feelings about the smoking issue—not to mention the deteriorating status of the city—when Sam grabbed my hand and pulled me into a children's clothing store. It was a trendy store where yuppies shopped in order to dress their toddlers as reasonable facsimiles of themselves. All over the Upper West Side you saw toddlers running around in sixty-dollar Guess jeans.

I had never been in a children's store with a man before and was about to ask him whether he had children—a thought that had belatedly occurred to me—when he asked the sales clerk for the largest bib they had.

"A bib?" I asked him as the sales woman brought out a pile and set them on the counter.

"I figured it was a better idea than replacing your T-shirt," he said. "That way you can carry it in your purse and take it out every time you have an ice cream cone."

I backed away from him. "You think I'm going to wear a *bib*?"

"I think you'll look adorable in it," he said, grabbing it and holding it up to me.

"You're spilling ice cream on that, sir," the woman said to him.

"That's the point," Sam told her. "Don't bother wrapping it up, she'll wear it."

"I know you're older than me, but you don't have to treat me like a child," I said.

"Just think of me as your father."

"You're not *that* old."

Sam smiled. "I'm glad to hear it." He was already tying the bib around my neck and I was too amused to stop him.

"You think I'm going to walk down Columbus Avenue wearing this?" I asked him, and then I started to laugh. Sam laughed too, as did one of the customers. The sales clerk wasn't even smiling.

As we exited the store, me wearing a bib with a picture of a teddy bear holding a red balloon, I realized it had been some time since I had laughed so hard. And I could seldom remember ever laughing with Max. He took everything too seriously.

I stopped laughing abruptly and started to examine my feelings. I had guilt feelings for laughing when I was supposed to be brokenhearted. I *was* brokenhearted.

Reading me perfectly, Sam said, "Hey, the world didn't end just because your husband dumped you. Keep laughing. It's good for you."

"How do you know he did the dumping?"

"It's pretty easy to spot. The one who does the dumping seldom loses any sleep over it."

"I thought I'd be married to him for the rest of my life."

"Everyone thinks that, but what percentage actually works out?"

"I'm not very good at change."

"Look, is it so bad? Instead of being home in front of the tube with your spouse, you're having a great time eating ice cream on Columbus Avenue with a man who's not old enough to be your father."

"We didn't watch television."

"I'm just trying to cheer you up."

"I know. Thanks."

"You're welcome."

"You're older than Max."

"Of course I am. If he was my age, he would've been too smart to dump you."

"Thanks for the bib."

"It was just a joke. I really don't expect you to carry it around with you."

"Okay. Then thanks for making me laugh."

"It was my pleasure."

Chapter Five

Review/FILM
THE CAT FROM ANOTHER PLANET
By Ellie Thomas

You would have thought by this time that screen-writers would've run out of extraterrestrial subjects but that doesn't appear to be happening. In *The Cat from Another Planet*, Allen Morgan (Tom Lanks) is a normal yuppie, worried about nothing more than which new club is "in" and which investments are out. That is before feeding his cat one morning and having his cat tell him he'd prefer another brand of cat food. The only suspense in this film is trying to figure out why Tom Lanks agreed to appear in it. For all-out feline excitement, I recommend watching a Morris the Cat commercial instead. Even the special effects were disappointing as one could sense someone out of range of the camera stepping on the cat's tail in order to get him to open his mouth.

Rated PG

IT HAD BEEN ANOTHER sleepless night and another day of napping in the screening room. I was managing to stay awake now during the first five minutes of a movie. I kept telling myself that if the movie hooked me in the first five minutes—which a good movie is supposed to do—then I would then stay awake. It was doubtful, though. The way I was going I would've slept through a movie starring both Kevin Costner and Mel Gibson. Nude. Not even a sexy body could compete with my state of exhaustion.

The day after telling Sam about the room for rent, I saw Philippa when I got home from work. I had finally managed to locate the last remaining window fan in the city and I was hurrying to my room with it when she stopped me in the hall.

"I want to thank you, Ellie," she said.

"Oh. What for?"

"For recommending this place to Sam Wiley. He took the room and I think he's going to fit in fine."

There was a certain look in her eyes and a certain tone to her voice that led me to suspect she had more than a landlady's interest in Sam. That was okay with me. Sam was fun to be with but it was my husband I was obsessed with. Although it hadn't hurt my ego that he seemed to be interested, particularly since I basically still thought of him as Max's type. And if Sam could be interested, maybe Max would come to his senses.

"Are you two old friends?" she asked me.

"No. He was at that party I went to last week and then I ran into him on Columbus Avenue last night."

"Then you two aren't dating?"

"Philippa," I said, "if you're interested in him, go for it. I still feel very married. He seems like a really nice guy."

"I know," she said, "and there aren't many of those around. And the ones that are, are gay. He's not..." she said, letting her words trail off as she raised an eyebrow.

"Definitely not. Divorced, and wasn't happy about it."

Her face lit up and I realized for the first time that she wasn't any older than me. Somehow, being my landlady had made her seem older. Plus—and I don't know why this is, but it is—brunettes always seem older than blondes.

"He's awfully attractive," she said.

"Then you'd like my husband," I told her. "I've been informed that they're the same type."

"I like that type," said Philippa. "Usually they turn out to be chess players, though."

"I know, isn't that odd? I guess I like that type, too."

"I also like the blond beach-boy type."

I thought of my brother, Pete, who would be far more appreciated on the East Coast than he seemed to be on the West.

"Well, I just wanted to check with you," she said. "What's that, a window fan?"

"Yes."

"I hope you won't leave it on when you're not home. The electric bill is killing me this summer."

"I won't," I promised her, although I imagined she was making a nice profit off the rooms she was renting plus her healing practice on the side. If she couldn't afford an electric bill, who could?

I installed the window fan before I even kicked off my shoes. I found that if I stood right in front of it, it managed to dry the sweat on my face, but as soon as I moved away, I began sweating again. It was in the nineties for the thirteenth straight day with humidity to match. The newspapers were hinting at holes in the ozone layer and I was beginning to think there was something to that theory.

I was trying to decide whether I had enough energy to go out and get something to eat or whether I should settle for the package of Twinkies I had picked up at the deli on the way home. The knock on my door came before I had reached any conclusion.

"Come on in," I said, and the door opened and Sam was standing there. For some reason, he wasn't sweating, and that fact annoyed me. If someone in long pants, a long-sleeve T-shirt and a beard wasn't sweating, maybe something was wrong with me.

"What're you doing tonight?" he asked.

"Sitting in front of my fan."

"I've heard of people staying at home and sitting in front of their fire, but a fan?"

"A fan is the summer equivalent of a fire. Unless you have an air conditioner, in which case you can sit home in front of a fire during the summer."

"A friend of mine has a loft with white walls." He paused while I tried to figure out what he was talking about.

"I assume you're telling me that for some reason."

"I thought I'd run my film for you."

Three movies in one day? No way. "I'm really not up for it tonight, Sam."

"I may not be able to set something up again."

I slumped and made a big deal of wiping my sweaty forehead off with my hand. "I'm beat. And I've already seen two movies today."

"Then you shouldn't be beat, that means four hours sleep, doesn't it?"

"Four doesn't make it."

"I'd really like you to see it."

"I'd like to see it and I know I'd love it, but one more movie today would do me in."

"I'll buy you dinner."

The thought of dinner in an air-conditioned restaurant won out. The fan wasn't really making any difference in the temperature in my room. "Okay," I said.

"Bring your notebook and pen or whatever you use."

"What for?"

"Don't you usually take notes at screenings?"

"I'm not reviewing it," I said.

"Wouldn't you please? I'd like to add it to my collection." His eyes looked like my cocker spaniel's used to look when he begged me for food.

"Sam—"

"And we'll get Häagen Dazs on the way home."

Already the man knew how to bribe me.

WHEN WE GOT to the street, he started to hail a taxi. "Can't we just eat around here?" I asked.

"Eat?" He made it sound like a word in a foreign language he didn't understand.

"Yes, eat. Dinner."

"I thought we'd see the movie first."

"But I'm starving," I protested.

"No way. If I feed you first, you'll fall asleep during the movie."

I didn't tell him I fell asleep just as easily before lunch as after lunch. What I did tell him was that I had no intention of getting into a taxi.

"It's all the way down in Chelsea," he told me.

"Fine. We'll take the subway."

"Are you serious?"

"Sam, I've yet to get a taxi with the air-conditioning turned on. And when you ask them to put it on, they all give you the same story—it makes the engine overheat. Come on, the subway's great this year."

"I never take the subways."

"Well, you ought to start. It's the fastest way around the city."

"Aren't they dangerous?" At least he managed to look a trifle sheepish as he asked it.

I looked at him in amazement. "Aren't you the intrepid traveler who recently returned from the Amazon?"

"There's no muggers in the Amazon."

"Just headhunters, right?"

"They're not as bad as you hear."

"Neither are the muggers," I said.

"You're determined to take the subway?"

"It's the only way to travel."

As we went down the steps to the entrance on Ninety-Sixth Street, he acted as though he were descending into the jaws of hell.

Sam followed me reluctantly through the turnstile, looking around with trepidation. I got the idea he hadn't spent much time in New York. The people he was trying to stay clear of were just the usual, ordinary subway riders whom I saw every day. People like me. I turned right on the platform and led him to the end where the first car would stop.

"I don't feel any air-conditioning," said Sam.

"The stations aren't air-conditioned, just the trains," I said, leaning over the track to see if a train was coming. Sam about had a heart attack over that and pulled me back, but not before I had seen the lights in the distance.

"Where're you from?" I asked him.

"You mean originally?"

"Before the Amazon."

"Colorado."

The train roared into the station, drowning out any more questions I might have. Colorado fit. The wild hair and the beard made more sense now. Instead of giving him the New York radical look that Max sported, it was more the look of a mountain man. As we got on the train I was trying to picture him in hiking boots and a flannel shirt climbing in the Rockies. Yes, that would be exactly the sort of person who would go to the Amazon. He probably didn't even know he looked like a New York intellectual.

"Where'd you go to school?" I asked him.

"Columbia University."

Well, maybe he did know.

"Why New York?"

"It's a great film school."

"Oh. I went to NYU."

"Pretty good school," he said, grinning at me. The film schools of the two universities were very competitive, rather like UCLA and SC. Columbia's, however, was known for being more intellectual and more into theory, while NYU produced more directors.

The train started up. Sam took a seat and I beat out a teenager for the place at the front where the only thing that was between me and the tunnel was a sheet of glass. It was like being in another world riding the subway in the front like that. It made me feel like I was hurtling through dark space on a roller-coaster ride.

"Don't you want to sit down?" asked Sam as the train started up.

"No."

I felt him join me and moved over to give him room to look. He didn't say anything until we pulled out of Seventy-second Street. From there to Forty-second Street it was nonstop and my favorite stretch of subway. A few years before there had been criticism of the engineers on the Seventh Avenue IRT line, some being likened to cowboys. There was supposed to be some kind of speed limit, but the engineers seemed to ignore it. Sometimes it felt as though we were going a hundred miles an hour, the engineer hurtling around curves and not applying the brakes until he started to pull into Forty-second Street, the fast braking often causing passengers to tumble over each other or hang on to the poles for dear life. It had the same appeal that drag racing had had when I was a teenager.

I heard a tale of woe start up behind me and saw Sam turning around to listen. This was a panhandler I was familiar with. He claimed to have just about every disease known to man and no health insurance. Once he caught my eye and tried to sell me his ragged tennis shoes. He had been drunk that particular morning and the smell of the booze combined with the odor that came from his feet when he removed his shoes and held them out to me made most of the passengers move to the other end of the car. That was in the days before he got such stiff competition from all the individuals claiming to be sick. Then he just asked for money for a drink. I was interested to see that the times had caught up with him and he'd changed his story.

Sam, obviously an easy sell, was digging into his pocket for some money. I felt like telling him to save it for someone more credible but didn't want to stifle his Good Samaritan impulse. New York could use all the Good Samaritans it could get.

We got off the train at Twenty-third Street and walked west to Eighth Avenue before heading downtown. I hadn't been in this area in some time and was surprised to see all the new restaurants and bars that had sprung up.

The last time I had been there it had been rather dingy; now it looked like it was in competition with Amsterdam Avenue to see which could be gentrified the quickest.

"Why'd you ask where I was from?" Sam asked me.

"You didn't seem familiar with subways."

"I'm in New York quite a bit. It's just that I usually walk wherever I'm going."

"Did you enjoy it?"

"*Enjoy* it? What's to enjoy about the subway?"

"Well, it saved us a seventy-three block walk in the heat, for one thing."

"I don't like to be under the ground. I'm not big on being in the air, either. When at all possible, I like to have my feet right on the earth's surface."

"You must fly a lot when you make your documentaries."

"I do, but I never enjoy it."

I gave him a look of glee. "You're afraid of flying?"

"I didn't say I was afraid. I just don't like it."

"What do you do on a plane to get over this dislike of yours?"

"I drink."

"You are afraid."

"It just relaxes me, that's all."

"I would think climbing a mountain would be a lot scarier than flying. Hanging out in space like that with only a rope to hang on to."

Sam gave me a baffled look. "What are you talking about?"

"Mountain climbing."

"What makes you think I climb mountains?"

"You said you were from Colorado."

"You certainly jump to conclusions fast, don't you?"

"You didn't live in the mountains?"

"I lived in Denver, and it's in the mountains, yes. I never climbed a mountain, though. I skied down mountains, but I never climbed up."

"Would you be afraid to climb a mountain?"

"No, I wouldn't be afraid. The idea just never appealed to me."

"It doesn't hurt to admit your fears, Sam. It doesn't make you any less of a man."

Sam stopped dead in the middle of the sidewalk and grabbed me by the shoulders. "Don't tell me I'm with someone who's been in deep analysis for ten years?"

"No. I've never been in analysis."

"Then what is it with you?"

"You're a little intimidating, that's all."

"Me?"

"I'd be scared to death to go near the Amazon."

"So it's *your* fears we're talking about."

"How can you stand all the insects?"

"It's the *insects* I go down to film."

"Aren't you afraid of anything?"

"Yeah. Movie critics." He let go of my shoulders and laughed. I loved his laugh. It was like a deep rumble coming out of the earth. He had a volcanic laugh that just erupted.

Sam turned right on Nineteenth Street and stopped at the second building from the corner. It was the kind of building that used to be industrial but had recently been converted to living lofts. He rang one of the buzzers on the street and the door was buzzed open.

We got in a do-it-yourself elevator and Sam pressed the button for the top floor. When the elevator opened, a short man in jogging gear stood there. He was halfway to being bald and had the face of a middle-aged man on the body of a teenager who worked out a lot. "You made good time," he said to Sam.

"We took the subway," said Sam.

"*You*? On the *subway*?"

Sam ignored the jibe. "This is Ellie Thomas, Josh—New York's finest film critic. Ellie, my old Columbia film school buddy, the great Josh Marra in person."

"Ellie who?" asked Josh, shaking my hand.

"Ignore him," I said. "I only review horror films and documentaries for *Views*."

"I never read reviews," said Josh.

"Josh is a film editor," said Sam.

The name clicked in. "You're Joshua Marra?"

He looked pleased at the recognition. "You've heard of me?"

"Sure. I've even said nice things about you in my reviews."

"Maybe I'll start reading *Views*," said Josh.

Josh had the projector all set up, had set out a couple of cold beers, and told us he'd be back after he ran six miles.

"Indoors?" I asked him, worried he was going to die of heat exhaustion.

"At the 'Y' on Twenty-third," he told me.

The loft was enormous and almost empty. I ignored the comfortable looking leather couch facing the wall on which the movie would be projected, and instead dragged over a straight-backed chair.

"I'm not going to bother you on the couch," said Sam. "Make yourself comfortable."

"I figure I'll stay awake better in this chair."

"Come on, Ellie, it's only seven-thirty at night and you haven't eaten yet. How could you go to sleep?"

I felt like saying, "Watch me." I was determined, however, to stay awake. I couldn't be so insulting as to sleep through his film twice.

Sam went around closing all the blinds on the windows, which made the loft dim but not dark. It also made it hot. If there was air-conditioning, I didn't feel it.

What I saw of the movie was charming. The camera zoomed in on a close-up of these incredible army ants eating a path through the jungle. In his narration, Sam likened them to Sherman's Army wending a path of destruction through the South. I remember laughing out loud at one point, and the next thing I knew, Sam was shaking my shoulder and yelling in my ear.

"Could you try to stay awake?"

"Sorry," I said, blinking at the screen.

"Look, why don't you sit on my lap. That ought to make you nervous enough to stay awake."

I shook my head and reached for the beer, but he grabbed it out of my hand. "No beer for you. You want a cold shower? Would that help?"

"Sam, I'm averaging two hours sleep a day. There's nothing that's going to keep me awake."

"Stand up."

"What?"

"I defy you to fall asleep standing up."

"I could probably fall asleep standing on my head."

"Try it. I'll run it upside down."

"I don't know how to stand on my head."

I decided he didn't need the hard time I was giving him, so I stood up and walked over behind the couch. It was something I should've thought of before. Certainly no one would object if I stood during screenings. On the other hand, I really needed those naps.

Guess what? It's quite possible to sleep standing up. After shaking me awake for the third time, Sam gave it up and turned off the projector.

"Please don't take it personally," I said. "I really loved what I saw."

"I'm not taking it personally. I just feel bad you're walking around like a zombie."

"So I'll be a zombie for eighteen months. Isn't that how long you said it took?"

"I'm going to make sure you sleep tonight."

"No sleeping pills," I told him. "I don't want to start that."

"I don't believe in pills," he said. "But I have this jungle remedy that I guarantee will work."

"I have a better idea," I said. "Maybe Josh would let me sleep on his couch with the projector running all night. Movies seem to be the only thing that put me to sleep."

"Why don't you just leave your TV on?"

"I don't have a TV."

"Rent one."

Another good idea, and one I'd try if his jungle remedy didn't work.

Sam left a note thanking Josh and we found a salad bar on Eighth Avenue. It was too hot to eat anything else. While we ate he told me more about army ants than I ever wanted to know. It seemed they would march right through the native's houses on stilts and the Indians would just move out of the way because there was no stopping them. If I saw something like that coming, I'd move out of the country. Sam had an interest in insects I didn't share.

"Do they bite?" I asked him.

"Of course they bite. I told you, they eat everything in their path."

"Including people?"

"If people are stupid enough to get in their way. The bites really sting. I got bit on the hand by one of them and it instantly swelled up and hurt like hell. This Indian guide of mine pulled off a leaf and told me to rub it, and it went away like magic."

"I'd die."

"No, you wouldn't."

"Believe me, I would."

"How can you say you like my films when you hate insects so much?"

"I like lots of things on film I don't like in real life."

"So what are you scared of, besides insects?"

"Alligators. Piranhas. Headhunters. Flying bats."

"Then you better stay away from the Amazon."

I didn't need Sam to tell me that.

SAM TOLD ME he'd be right back with the magic potion. That was exactly what I was expecting, some kind of magic potion.

When he arrived at my room with a large glass in his hand, however, my first taste told me it had a high percentage of alcohol.

"This is booze," I complained, after having choked on the first swallow.

"Damn right," said Sam.

"You want me to get *drunk* to get to sleep?"

"It always worked for me in the jungle."

"I don't feel like waking up with a hangover every morning."

"I've got just the thing for a hangover, too."

"What? More booze?"

"Why do you always have to give me an argument?"

"I don't know."

"I'm not your husband. I'm just trying to help you out, you know."

"I know and I appreciate it."

"If you're going through an I-hate-men period, I understand. I wasn't so big on women for a long time after my divorce."

"I don't think I hate men."

"I guess it would be understandable."

"Sam, I don't hate you!"

"You don't have to yell at me."

"It's just that you're so nice, so damn understanding. It gets on my nerves."

"Wasn't your husband nice to you?"

"Dammit, will you just forget about him?"

"I wonder what's bringing on this little fit of temper."

"*You're* bringing it on."

"How can I forget about him?" he asked. "You're still married to him and you'll probably go back to him."

"I wouldn't be so sure."

"What does that mean?"

"I don't know. I'm confused. I don't get any sleep anymore." I practically wailed the last few words.

Sam leaned down and kissed me on the top of the head. "Look, if you want to sleep, drink it. If you don't, stay awake all night. It's your decision." He went back out and closed my door before I could tell him to take his drink with him.

Five minutes later he walked out of his room and saw me sitting on the floor outside my bathroom, waiting my turn at the shower. He walked down and stood over me.

"You sleeping in the hall tonight?" he asked me.

"Someone's in the shower."

He gestured with his head towards his bathroom at the other end of the hall. "Go on, be my guest."

"I can use your shower?"

"Just don't leave your wet towel on the floor."

"I won't. I never do. I take my towel back to my room with me."

"I was just kidding, Ellie, Leave your towel anywhere you want."

"Thank you, I really appreciate it," I told him.

I sneaked a look in Sam's medicine cabinet while I was in there. Some people think they can tell about another person by seeing what books are in the bookcases; I always look in medicine cabinets. I know too many people who buy books they never read, but I don't know anyone who stocks their medicine cabinet just to impress their guests.

Sam's cabinet had exactly two items: a much-used blue toothbrush and a much-squeezed tube of Colgate. No shaving items, no medications; it didn't look like he even got headaches. I was impressed. For minimalistic medicine cabinets, he had everyone I knew beat. I kept more than that in my desk drawer at work, and I didn't even spend much time in the office. Max and I had each had our own medicine cabinet in the bathroom and both of them were constantly overflowing. Sam was either the healthiest man I'd ever known or had the least sense. Or maybe he just hadn't unpacked yet.

I hadn't planned on drinking the concoction he had fixed me. I ended up drinking it, though, and it worked. Right afterward I was having this new revenge fantasy. Max and Jean were once again cavorting in the nude around our living room, but this time, just out of sight, about a billion army ants were creeping up on them. The last thing I remembered were the army ants turning into the living room and heading in their direction.

It was to become one of my favorite fantasies.

Chapter Six

Review/FILM
THEY KILL IN THE SUBWAYS
by Ellie Thomas

The producer/director/writer who brought us *They Kill in the Dark*, *They Kill in the Alleys* and *They Also Kill on 747'S*, must have felt that we were ready for *They Kill in the Subways*. I was not ready. Now I like vampires as much as the next person, and Stung can bite my throat anytime, but these particular vampires looked underage and ineffective and not nearly as scary as some ordinary subway denizens I run into every day. Despite amazing special effects from George Simon and his team, the most amazing thing about this film is that it was actually shot in New York City subways and no one in the cast or crew got killed. For real excitement, I would suggest skipping this movie and going for a ride on the IND line after midnight instead.

Rated PG

THE ALCOHOLIC POTION worked. I slept soundly straight through the night and midway into the morning. The only thing was I woke with a terrific hangover. Still, the hangover made my conscious mind forget how miserable my subconscious was and so I greeted my hangover like a long lost friend. I also rewarded it with coffee and doughnuts at the first opportunity.

On my way to work I stopped in a neighborhood store and made arrangements to rent a television set and a VCR. I would henceforth conduct my own private screenings in bed at night, and if that didn't put me to sleep, nothing would. Just the opening credits of a film now seemed to signal sleep to my body. Sixty-five dollars a month was nothing to me if it meant I would once again be sleeping through the night.

I stopped by the newspaper office before my first screening and found Woody and several of the others lying in wait for me.

"Good morning, folks," I said to them, although it was still barely morning by that time.

"Ellie," said Woody, "about your review yesterday." Behind Woody, three of my colleagues were gathered in close. They reminded me of vultures waiting for the body. I deduced that I was today's carrion.

"What about it?" I asked.

"It's just that... Oh, hell, Ellie, what's happening to you? You've always loved his movies."

"Are we getting bribes now, Woody, to give them good reviews?" In unison, the vultures' heads shifted to look at Woody.

"All the other papers loved it. Siskel and Ebert gave it two thumbs up." The vultures turned back to me.

"I call them as I see them," I said.

"That's just it, Ellie," said Woody. "I've been hearing rumors that you've been sleeping through the screenings.'' The vultures looked aghast. Not that some of them didn't routinely sleep through screenings.

"Nonsense," I said, as the vultures moved in closer.

"Hey, guys, give us some room," said Woody, taking my arm and hustling me into his office. Through his door I watched the vultures drift in the direction of the coffee machine.

Woody's office fan was busily blowing hot air around the room. "Can you believe this weather, Ellie?"

"Not really. It feels more like August than June."

"I hear it's a hole in the ozone layer. It's beginning to look like time to move to Canada."

I would have liked to keep weather as the subject, but I knew that sooner or later Woody would get back to my reviews, so I might as well go on the offense. "What do you want me to do, Woody? Give good reviews to bad movies?"

Woody put on his concerned look. "I think you ought to take some time off, El."

"I don't want to take any time off. I need to work right now."

"What're you scheduled to see today?"

"*Varsity Werewolves.*"

"No wonder you're falling asleep in the screenings."

"I think I can guarantee I'll be awake during this one," I said, feeling refreshed after ten hours sleep.

"How can you be so sure?"

"Hey, Woody, you know I love football."

NOT EVEN THE NOVELTY of watching football in June kept me awake, however. One good night's sleep didn't make up for all the missed nights, and ten minutes into the movie I was snoring so loudly Meredith had to keep poking me. She said I was the most entertaining thing about the movie.

"That bad?" I asked.

"Worse."

"You going to tell me about it?"

"Believe me, Ellie, anything you make up is going to sound better than anything I could tell you. I can't believe I actually do this for a living."

"Would you give me a hint?"

"The title tells it all. Just think football and werewolves and you've pretty much got the picture."

"Was there anything redeeming about it? Special effects? Sound track?"

"Nothing. We're talking really low budget here."

"Were the werewolves at least scary?"

"You know those wax teeth you can buy at Halloween?"

I nodded.

"I think that's what they used. I've seen six-year-olds in costumes that looked scarier."

"Any good up-and-coming actors in it? The next generation of Brat Packers?"

"Nary a one."

"Will the kids like it?"

"Are you kidding? It'll probably gross twenty-five million the first weekend. Another trashy, guaranteed hit."

THE APARTMENT was quiet and everyone appeared to be out. I stopped by Sam's room on the off chance that he would be there and I could thank him for the night's sleep, but he was out, too.

I decided to take a different tack with my reviews. I'd start giving them rave reviews, which would take even more creativity on my part and possibly satisfy Woody in the bargain.

The TV and VCR were delivered and the guy set them up on the floor opposite my couch for me. It made me feel like I was getting away with something to have a television set. Max considered TV to be the greatest evil of the twentieth century, ahead of air pollution and nuclear waste. It felt like I was playing hookey from school having the TV on during the day. I quickly tuned in to a soap opera.

I was watching Phil Donahue when the phone rang. I turned down the sound in case it was Max calling to beg me to come back to him. He'd kill me if he knew I had a television set.

It was Alicia.

"How're you enjoying single life?" she asked me.

"I don't feel single."

"That's not what I hear. I hear you and Sam have moved in together."

"What?"

"You know you can't keep a secret on the Upper West Side. It's like a small town."

"You heard wrong, Alicia. I told Sam about a room available where I'm renting, that's all."

"You want to know where I heard it?"

"You must have run into Sam."

"No, no—I have my sources. As a matter of fact, my healer told me."

"You go to Philippa?"

"Why didn't you tell me you were living in her apartment?"

"It didn't occur to me."

"She's marvelous. You know she's rated second in the world for psychic healing?"

"I can't believe you go to a healer."

"Listen, she's cheaper than a doctor."

"Are you okay?"

"I am now. You know I used to get migraines?"

"I don't remember you getting migraines."

"They must have started after I married Richard. Actually, they probably started *because* I married Richard. Anyway, as soon as I feel one coming on, I call Philippa, she comes over, and that's it for the migraine."

"That's amazing. She must be good."

"She's marvelous. You ought to get something just so she can heal it."

"The only thing I have is insomnia and I think I found a cure for it this afternoon."

"Sleeping pills?"

"Television."

"Oh, yes, that should do it. So tell me, you seeing Sam tonight?"

"I'm not *seeing* Sam, Alicia."

"He's a very sweet man."

"Yes, he is."

"Still—" and I could hear her trying not to laugh "—you don't want to run from man to man."

"I didn't run from Max; he threw me out."

"You should have run from him the first time you met him."

"Alicia—"

"Well, since you're not seeing him, how about meeting me for dinner? Richard's working late and I forgot to defrost anything."

"Something light. You up for Japanese?"

"Always."

We arranged to meet at seven, which gave me time to watch two full hours of news before it was time to leave to meet her.

Columbus Avenue has some nice sidewalk cafés but it was too hot that night to even think of sitting outside. We managed to get the last table in the smoking section of a new sushi restaurant where the guy who had delivered my TV waved to me from the bar.

"Cute guy," observed Alicia.

"He's just the guy who delivered my TV. I rented a TV and VCR since Max is no longer around to disapprove."

"That's what I like to hear, a show of independence."

"I want to join a video club and rent a movie tonight."

"I'll take you by mine after we've eaten. It only costs twenty dollars to join for a year."

"Sounds good."

"They have the new Kevin Costner movie in. If you haven't seen it, I guarantee you'll love it. I wouldn't mind renting it again."

"Alicia, I'm getting a movie to sleep to, not watch."

"Oh, yeah, I forgot."

We were finishing our salads when Alicia said, "You know those stories I told you I was writing?"

"Yes. I'd love to see them sometime."

"I read one aloud to Richard last night."

"So what did he think?"

"You're not going to believe this."

"What?"

"He laughed." She gave me this deadpan look that looked very much like Richard.

"Richard laughed?"

"He does occasionally."

"Was it supposed to be funny?"

"That's the strange thing. I thought it was amusing, but I didn't think someone would laugh out loud."

"It was probably you. You can be pretty funny."

"Me?"

"Yes, the way you say things sometimes. You used to make me laugh all the time."

"But you're the one who writes funny."

"And I'm never funny when I say anything."

The sushi came and Alicia fooled with hers for a minute, not really eating any. Then she said, "Richard thinks I ought to do it as performance art."

"Oh, God, don't you hate that pretentious stuff they pass off as performance art?"

Alicia looked affronted.

"I don't mean you."

"I know what you mean, El. Yes, I do hate it. But I like Spaulding Grey."

"I don't mean him. I like him, too."

"Well, that's kind of what Richard means. A cross between Spaulding Grey and a standup comic, I guess. There's this activist church in the Village with a coffee shop—"

"On Washington Square?" Alicia nodded. "I know it. I went to see some folk singers there."

"That's the place. Anyway, we know the people who run it and they said I could try it out there next month. I guess I'll find out whether anyone besides Richard laughs."

"You're really going to do it?"

"I'm thinking about it."

"Would you have the guts to do it?" I couldn't remember Alicia ever liking to be the center of attention. She wouldn't even act in one of my student films.

"I don't know. I've never performed in front of people. I'm not scared, though, although maybe I should be."

"You have guts, Alicia. I'd die. Can I come?"

"Only if you promise to laugh."

"Of course I'll laugh."

"That wasn't what I wanted to talk to you about, though," she said.

"I just thought you were being sociable," I said.

"I *am* being sociable. I'd like to see more of you, which is why I immediately thought of you when this came up."

"What came up?"

"Listen, are you seeing Scott?"

"No, I'm not seeing Scott."

"Oh, I thought he was interested."

"I went out with him once and it was a disaster. All he does is talk about himself."

"That's all Max ever did."

"No, there's a difference. Max liked to spout his film theories, but Scott spends a great deal of time talking about his skin. And his hair. And his muscle tone."

"Well, he's got pretty good skin and hair and muscle tone."

"I'm not interested in Scott, Alicia. Is that what you wanted to talk to me about?"

"No. It's just that if you were seeing him, you'd probably be spending your weekends on Fire Island."

"It's not worth it."

"Good, because Richard and I and another couple have a share in a house at the New Jersey Shore for the summer. There was a third couple, but they just backed out. We have it for alternate weekends beginning this Saturday."

"And you want me to take their place."

"Would you want to? It would be great, Ellie. We have so much to catch up on."

"How much?"

"Four thousand."

Naturally it had to be the exact amount I had left in the bank. "I don't know, Alicia. I think if I were going to go away somewhere I'd rather go to the country."

"It's right on the beach."

"I grew up on the beach; it's no big deal."

"But don't you miss it?"

"I guess. Sometimes."

"According to the weatherman on TV tonight, this is going to be the hottest summer on record. Maybe you can spend your summer sitting inside in your air-conditioned room, but that's about all you'll be able to do."

"My room isn't air-conditioned."

"No air-conditioning?"

"Philippa says the wiring in the building won't take it."

"I'd get her to heal the wiring."

She made me laugh. "You ought to do one of those stories about Philippa," I said. "That could be really funny."

"So you want to take the share?"

"I don't know. I'm kind of in the mood to be a miserable martyr in the city all summer."

"Who's that going to impress...Max? He won't even know."

I thought of long swims, cool ocean beaches, not having to wait in line for the bathroom. "How many bedrooms does it have?"

"Three."

I could hear the sound of sea gulls and waves lapping up on the shore.

Alicia said, "You'll have a built-in social life. You'll probably even meet some men."

"I'm really not feeling social."

She played what I'm sure she thought was her best card. "Bring Sam out. You can have the room with the two twin beds."

I was instantly suspicious. "Why would I want to bring Sam out?"

"Everyone likes Sam and he'd probably like to get out of the city, too."

"Then talk Sam into the share."

"I can find someone to buy the share, Ellie. I was just hoping it would be you. I guess I'm so glad to see you again that I want to see more of you."

"I don't know, Alicia."

"Did you and Max ever get a share in a place?"

"Not Max. he was too cheap to pay rent on two places at the same time."

"Think how aggravated he'd be if he found out you had a summer place."

"Wouldn't he, though." What a tempting thought.

"It's so pretty there, Ellie, and much cooler than the city. The most beautiful, clean beaches—well, I guess you're used to clean beaches in California."

"We got oil spills occasionally."

"You don't even have to take the bus—you can drive out with us on Friday nights."

"What makes you think I can afford it?"

Alicia looked stricken. "Oh, Ellie, I'm sorry. Forget I even mentioned it. Listen, we can have guests on the Fourth of July. You can come out with us then."

"Actually, I happen to have exactly four thousand dollars in the bank. I might need it if I find an apartment, though."

"Can't you save out of your salary?"

"I guess." I thought of Max calling me and asking me to have a drink with him some weekend and me telling him that I couldn't, that I was going to my beach house. That might be a better form of revenge than anything I had previously planned. "Okay," I said, "I'll do it. And I'll write you a check now before I can change my mind."

"And bring out Sam."

"I kind of hate to monopolize him. I think Philippa's interested in him."

"I gathered that. Which is why you better make your move."

"My *move*? I'm still married, you know. Anyway, I distinctly remember you telling me I should go for a different type this time. Like Scott."

"Oh, I just thought you could have some fun with Scott. Sam really isn't anything like Max; they just look similar. Everyone likes Sam. And he's easy to be around and he knows the other couple."

"Do I know the other couple?"

"I don't think so. Do you know Claire and Josh?"

"Is he an editor?"

"They both are."

"A loft in Chelsea?"

"I didn't know you knew Josh."

"I don't. Sam introduced me to him. He let us screen Sam's film in his loft."

"Claire's an editor, too. They don't live together, but they've been going together for years."

"I'll need a new bathing suit."

"It's very casual there. We don't dress up like they do in the Hamptons."

"Not casual enough for what I've got. The elastic's shot and I'm in danger of losing it the next time I wear it."

"This is going to be great, Ellie. I'm so glad we're in touch again."

"I am, too," I told her. "Is it okay with Richard?"

"Richard's crazy about you. It was Max he didn't like."

"Are you sure?"

"Look, I know you were never crazy about Richard, but he isn't so bad. I know he used to be pompous about the theater in the old days, but he's lightened up considerably since directing on TV."

When I thought about it, I had never minded Richard. In fact I quite liked him until Max influenced me with all his criticism of him. And the criticism was probably over jealousy of my friendship with Alicia more than anything else.

"There's one thing I better warn you about," Alicia said. "You know the stories I was telling you about?"

"What about them?"

"They're personal."

"You told me."

"What I didn't tell you is that a lot of people I know are in them. I change the names, but you'll be able to recognize yourself."

"*I'm* in it?"

"Not as much as Richard."

"You're telling funny stories about *me*?"

"I'm telling funny stories about me, and you happen to be in some."

"Okay. I don't mind."

"Maybe you better wait until you hear them. I was thinking maybe I could practice them on you at the shore this weekend."

"I'm looking forward to it." And I was. The worst summer of my life might not turn out as badly as I thought it would.

I JOINED ALICIA'S video club and took out *Lost Boys*, one of my favorite movies. I was almost to my room when Sam's door opened and he stuck his head out. "How'd you sleep last night?" he asked me.

I gave him a big smile. "Very well, thanks to you."

"Did you have a hangover?"

"Of course I had a hangover, but it was worth it. Do you know I slept ten consecutive hours?"

He looked pleased. "Good enough. You want another?"

"I rented a TV instead," I told him, holding up my video.

"Well, if it doesn't work, you know where to come for another jungle special."

"Meet me in the kitchen in ten minutes," I said to him. "I want to ask you something."

"That sounds interesting. Of course it would sound more interesting if you said to meet you in your room."

I gave him a look guaranteed to put a stop to that kind of talk, then went into my room. I took a quick shower while the bathroom was free, then headed for the kitchen in Max's old, soft flannel robe that I had appropriated from him early on in our marriage.

For some reason, Sam was fixing us hot chocolate. "It's too hot for cocoa," I said.

"The hot milk should help you sleep."

"I'm hoping a movie will do it."

"It doesn't hurt to cover all your bets."

I sat down at the table and waited for him to finish. When we were both sitting down drinking our cocoa, I said, "I had dinner with Alicia tonight. She talked me into taking a share on their beach house at the Jersey shore."

"Getting out of the city should be good for you."

"Alicia said to invite you out for the weekend if you want to come."

"Alicia suggested it? I didn't know she knew we knew each other."

"Philippa told her."

"Our landlady?"

"It seems she's Alicia's healer."

"This gets more and more complicated."

"Look, you're invited if you want to come. Your friend Josh and his girlfriend have the other share."

"This is a little sudden," he said.

"What's a little sudden?"

"You inviting me to spend the weekend with you. Are you sure you're ready for it?"

"I'm inviting you as a friend, Sam. I'm told we'll have the room with the twin beds. For that matter, there's probably a couch you can sleep on."

He gave a big sigh of relief. "That's better. I don't think we should rush things."

"There's nothing to rush. I thought we could be friends, that's all."

"You had me scared there for a minute."

"Will you stop it?"

He grinned. "I love getting a rise out of you."

He teased me in a way Max never had and I wasn't used to it. It was kind of nice, though. Brotherly.

"What's this costing you?"

"Four thousand."

"I'll pay half."

"I'd rather you didn't," I said.

"I'd feel better if I did."

"I'd rather it were my share. Then if I want to invite someone else, I can."

"You mean this is a one-weekend deal? Then I get replaced?"

"Sam, if you want a share in a house, get your own."

"You'll probably be inviting that young actor next. The one with the blond curls."

"I know which one you're talking about."

"If you can tear him away from his tanning machine."

"I do not want to invite that young actor."

"I guess I'll have to be satisfied with one weekend."

"Will you cut it out? I hardly know you. I just thought you might like to get out of the city for the weekend and you'll know everyone there."

"I'll get a ride out with Josh."

"We can drive out with Alicia and Richard after work Friday. They offered us a ride."

"I can't. Josh is going to screen my film for Philippa Friday night. She expressed an interest in seeing it."

"Philippa?"

"Our landlady."

"I know who Philippa is." And she sure hadn't wasted any time. Not that we were in a contest.

"Unlike some people, I fully expect her to stay awake during the screening," said Sam.

"Is she going to write a review of it, too?"

"No, but I figure if there're any bad parts, she'll heal them."

"A psychic editor?"

"Something like that."

"Are you taking her out to dinner, too?"

"Hey, listen, you've got to keep in good with land-ladies, don't you know that?"

"She gets enough rent—"

"You told me it was a good deal."

I stood up and carried my cup over to the sink. "Well, have fun, and I'll see you out there on Saturday. And please explain to Philippa that we're just friends."

He gave me a sunny smile. "I already did."

For some reason, that didn't go down well. It wasn't jealousy so much as a competitive nature, and part of me thought they'd get on very well together. The other part, though, felt somewhat rejected, the way I had felt when Max had left me for Jean. But at least it would be easier to be friends with him, and I needed all the friends at the moment that I could get.

"Sleep well," he called out to me as I walked out of the kitchen.

Chapter Seven

Review/FILM
VARSITY WEREWOLVES
By Ellie Thomas

This is unusual summer fare for teenagers in that there is no moral to the story. The first-string varsity football team of Rockland High School is, for some unexplained reason, composed entirely of teenage werewolves. We see cheerleaders and fans alike going crazy over this football team that really demolishes their competition. In one grisly, graphic scene after another, opposing players are torn limb from limb. Despite the overabundance of violence, however, the film also has its humorous and its touching moments. One such moment is when the werewolf quarterback (Jeff Ridges) fakes a hand-off, runs with the ball, throws a lateral pass on the five-yard line and then hugs his running back who has gone in for the touchdown. The poignancy of this scene brought real tears to this reviewer's eyes. Bravo to the director, Costa Brava, and let's hope that there will soon be a sequel to *Varsity Werewolves*.

Rated R

THE VIEW out my bedroom window looked shot with a filtered lens. Having grown up on the beach, I knew it was due to fog rolling in. I was hoping that the fog in New Jersey, like Southern California, would burn off by midmorning as I was looking forward to a beach day. The thing about beach houses was, if there wasn't any sun, there wasn't anything to do, and I was hoping to get in some serious body surfing.

I was glad enough of the little bit of daylight coming in; it was the hours in the darkness when I couldn't fall asleep that I hadn't much liked. When the sun came up I didn't feel as alone. There's something about lying awake in the middle of the night, in the dark, that makes you think you're the only one in the world not asleep. Or at least the only one not asleep who wants to be asleep.

We had stopped to eat on the road the night before and by the time we got to the house it was late. I unpacked my stuff in my room. Alicia was wrong about there being twin beds. Instead, there were bunkbeds. My brothers had had bunk beds and I had always wanted them, and the thought of sleeping in the top bunk seemed like an adventure.

When I joined Alicia and Richard in the living room, Richard had just opened a bottle of wine. We planned what we'd do the next day—go to the beach, mostly—as we finished off the bottle. I was feeling relaxed and tired by the time Alicia suggested we turn in.

I was debating whether to ask Richard to carry the TV set I had spied in the corner into my bedroom, in order to help me get to sleep. I felt like I could get to sleep without it, but I'd been wrong about that before. I had just decided to ask him, when, without even being asked,

Richard got up and went to the TV set, picked it up and headed down the hall with it.

"Where's he going with that?" I asked Alicia, wondering whether Richard was psychic.

She shook her head. "Richard has gone from hating and loathing TV, to wanting it on when he goes to sleep at night. I wear ear plugs these days."

I didn't want to make a scene and demand the TV for myself, so instead I finished off the last of the wine in my glass as Alicia turned out the lights.

I was still feeling sleepy and mellow when my head hit the pillow. I told myself, *I will not think of Max, I will not think of revenge* which, of course, instantly fixed my mind on exactly that. I was off and running on my army ant fantasy and I soon lost count of how many times I directed those little ants into the living room and over the bodies of Max and Jean, whom they quickly devoured. This fantasy was completely satisfying, and I didn't seem to tire of it in its endless variations. There would be Max, his beard turned black by the ants, begging me to come back to him. There would be Jean, the ants covering her breasts so that she looked as though she had a hairy chest, begging my forgiveness and telling me that Max was just as boring in bed as her husband. There were both of them, covered by an enormous mountain of writhing ants in the middle of our living room floor, with faint cries of "Get the can of Raid, Ellie," coming from somewhere in the middle of the mountain.

I was still savoring my fantasies but I would rather have been savoring a good night's sleep. I stared at the fog rolling in as long as I could, then I got up and got dressed.

I was out in the kitchen having a cup of coffee when I heard a car drive up and then a door slam. A moment later Sam and Josh and Claire were entering the door. Claire was a good foot taller than Josh, a skinny redhead with a deep laugh. Sam introduced us before they joined me at the table for coffee. Josh opened up a bag of doughnuts he had been carrying and we all helped ourselves.

"What are you guys doing up so early?" I asked them. It was barely seven and it was a couple of hours drive from the city.

"Claire wanted a full day at the beach," said Josh.

"Let's change into our suits and march onto the sand like little army ants," said Claire.

"Relax, Claire, we just got here," said Josh.

"Oh?" said Claire. "And who got his six-mile run in before we even left the city?"

Like a spotlight, the sun suddenly burst through the kitchen window.

"See?" said Claire. "That's a sign."

"I was worried it was going to be foggy all day," I said.

"Hey, I like your reviews," Claire said to me.

"Thanks."

"Particularly lately. You're really getting bizarre. I can't wait to see *Varsity Werewolves*."

"You'll see it alone," said Josh.

"Don't go by her reviews," said Sam, "she's been sleeping through the screenings."

"It's supposed to be pure trash," I told her.

Claire grinned. "I love pure trash."

"You'd love my job, then."

"Come on, guys, let's go swimming," said Claire, but everyone ignored her.

"How'd the screening go last night?" I asked Sam, trying to sound only slightly interested. "Did Philippa like it?"

"It knocked her dead."

"You mean she fell asleep?"

"If I used those words to describe your reaction, that's what I'd mean, but Philippa was enthusiastic. She wants me to do a documentary on her holistic clinic."

"Are you going to?"

"No. All she really needs is a video and I'm not into that."

Claire excused herself from the table and was back in her bikini before we'd started on a second cup of coffee.

"I'm going for a swim," she announced. "Anyone want to join me?"

"Later," said Josh. "You're not supposed to swim after you eat."

"One doughnut doesn't count," said Claire, heading out the door.

We were on our third cup of coffee and third doughnut when Alicia and Richard finally rolled out of bed. The kitchen table would only seat four so we moved out onto the deck. The sun was out in full force now and it was already hot. I was glad I was at the beach and not in my room in Manhattan.

I saw Claire coming back across the beach toward us and her hair was still dry.

"Didn't you go swimming?" Josh asked her as she got within talking distance of the deck.

"Ugh," she said, almost spitting out the word.

"What's the matter?" Josh asked.

"I've never seen a more disgusting sight."

Josh laughed. "Claire can't stand the sight of fat old ladies in swimming suits. She thinks they should be banned from the beaches."

"There aren't any fat old ladies on the beach," said Claire. "In fact there isn't anyone except a couple of life guards. What there is is a multitude of hypodermic needles that have washed up on the sand, along with some other items that are too gross to even mention." She made barfing noises and crossed her eyes to us, reminding me of my brother Pete when he was about ten.

"It's polluted?" I asked.

"Totally," said Claire. "You can use part of the beach, but they're not allowing anyone within ten yards of the water."

"It's too hot on the beach if you can't go in the water," I said, already missing the swim I hadn't even had.

"We ought to demand our money back," said Richard.

"Let's wait and see if they get it cleaned up," said Claire.

"Cleaned up?" asked Richard. "God only knows what's still out in the water. Or what disease we could catch."

"I could name a few," said Josh.

"Well, let's see. What're we going to do today?" asked Sam, seeming to be less upset than the rest of us. I wondered if maybe he was afraid of the water.

"Are there any pools around here?" I asked.

"No," said Alicia. "Why would they build a pool when there's all that ocean?"

"Any malls?" I missed malls.

"There's a bunch of little trendy shops," said Richard, "with the same things you can buy in the city, but for twice as much."

"There's probably a ballgame on this afternoon," said Josh.

"I think we ought to get our money back," said Richard.

They didn't get it cleaned up and the water remained closed to the public for the entire weekend. Nevertheless, we had a good time. Everyone got sunburned but me. People expect me to burn because I'm blond, but for some reason, maybe because I was brought up on the beach in California, I always tan.

Saturday night Alicia did her stories for us. We sat around the living room while Alicia took center stage on the area rug. And without any more ado, she began to tell very personal stories about herself.

I was amazed from the start. I would've thought she'd been in front of an audience all her life. She walked around, she gestured, her expressive face mirrored her thoughts in the way all good actors' faces do. I looked at Richard and saw that he was as surprised as I was.

She started telling a little about her childhood, things she had never confided to me even though I could clearly remember talking deep into the night with her about all kinds of subjects.

"My father and mother," she said, "drank a lot. And when they drank, they fought. Dad would be screaming at my mother, waving his fists around and smashing anything they came in contact with, and since they usually fought in the kitchen, it was usually something breakable. Mother would be on her hands and knees, crawling across the kitchen floor, begging him to forgive her. My brother would be in the bedroom, making a bomb with his chemistry set in order to blow me up, and I'd be in the closet hiding."

I couldn't believe she was telling us such personal things. At first I think we were a little uneasy hearing it, but at some point we all started to laugh. It wasn't funny, but the way she told it was funny. Even her father's heart attack—which killed him—seemed funny. And the brother—and I knew how many years of analysis it took for Alicia to get over her fear of her brother—came out sounding like a harmless nut.

These were traumatic things she was talking about and yet she managed to get us laughing and, with a little revising, I thought, could keep us laughing. Some parts were slower than they needed to be and some parts could be cut out completely. The funniest, and even more personal part of the story, were her experiences with boys in college. I was in there, and she had changed my name, but I was easily recognizable nevertheless.

"So here I am," said Alicia, "this neurotic nineteen-year-old with about a zero in self-confidence, and who should I get for my roommate in college? A blonde, with a great tan, from Southern California. Were boys calling our room nonstop that year? Oh, yes, and all of them were calling Cindi. That was her name, Cindi. All female babies born in California are given names ending in *y* or *i*. It's a cultural thing out there."

She went on and on and it was very funny, but it could have been funnier. I could tell that she was trying to be overly kind to the other characters in her monologue, the ones with the thinly disguised names. I would rather it was funnier, though, even if it was me she was making fun of.

I was the blonde from the West Coast whom the boys were all trying to get to through Alicia. I hadn't realized that at the time and it made me feel bad now, even though I couldn't stop laughing while she was describing the situation. It was exaggerated, though. She had plenty of boys after her; it was just that she always preferred the ones after me. The grass always looks greener and all that.

"And then," she said, "when any sane girl would give up guys forever, who should come along but Robert. You think *I* was neurotic? Let me tell you about Robert. First of all, I was a film major and he was a theater major. Does that tell you something about how pretentious he was?"

I started laughing and then looked over at Richard. If he hadn't been laughing I would've stopped, but he seemed to have a better sense of humor about himself than I ever gave him credit for.

She went on for an hour. Once in a while she would glance at some notes she held in one hand, but most of the time she just talked to us smoothly, without any pauses or stumbling around. It was very professional and more entertaining than many productions I had seen in theaters. I also knew it could be improved, but I thought that what Alicia needed most tonight was a boost to her confidence.

Afterward she kept asking, "Did you really like it?" and we kept assuring her we did. I think we all could've kept listening to it for several hours. It was certainly better than anything on TV.

I wasn't sure what she could do with it other than put it on in coffee houses, but I did think that Alicia had finally found something that was exactly right for her, and I was a little bit jealous that I didn't have something like that.

"I'M SLEEPING on top."

"She doesn't mean that the way it sounds," Alicia said.

"I liked the way it sounded," said Sam.

"It's bunk beds," I told him. "And the top one's mine."

"Even I'm disappointed with that answer," said Richard.

"Did you sleep last night?" Sam asked me.

I shook my head.

"You didn't sleep at all?" asked Alicia.

I shrugged.

"Didn't you put the TV in your room?" asked Sam.

"I had the TV," said Richard. "I like it on when I go to sleep."

"But you can sleep without it, can't you?" Sam asked him.

"Sure. You want it in your room, Ellie?"

"It'll probably keep Sam awake," I said, hating such a fuss being made over me.

"I'm sleeping on the couch," said Sam. "You need sleep more than you need a bunk mate."

Since I hadn't seen a movie that day, I was totally exhausted. I ended sleeping in the lower bunk after all since I couldn't see the TV set from the top.

Richard tuned it in to an old, 1940s movie, and I fell asleep so fast I didn't even see the opening credits.

SUNDAY MORNING the thing happened that I had been waiting to happen. I just never would have expected it to happen in New Jersey.

We had fixed a huge breakfast and afterward, while Richard and Claire took their turns cleaning up, Sam and I took a walk down the beach. It was deserted of people except for one lone couple about a mile away who were walking in our direction.

Even when the other couple got close enough so that they began to look familiar to me, no warning sounded. Probably because the last place I expected to see Max and Jean was in New Jersey.

So there I was, innocently walking with Sam, not expecting to see anything more exciting than perhaps a hypodermic needle imbedded in the sand, when the distance between us and the other couple closed to a few yards and I finally realized who it was.

My eyes zoomed in on them, focused, and I swore out loud.

"What's the matter?" asked Sam. "Did you step on something?"

"My husband," I muttered.

"You stepped on your husband?"

"That man. Walking toward us. That's my husband."

"You're kidding."

"I wish I were."

"You going to fall apart on me?"

"I hope not."

"Listen, be cool. Introduce us. Act as though he's just a casual acquaintance, someone you can hardly be bothered to recognize."

"Right," I murmured, wishing a tidal wave would arrive to sweep us off to sea.

They were now close enough so that I could see the shocked looks of surprise on their faces. Well, shock and surprise on Max's—Jean looked ready to die of embarrassment. *Wonderful* I thought. *I hope she does.*

"Good morning," I said casually, prepared to walk right by them. I had managed the "good morning," but I wasn't sure I could manage anything else.

Max stopped dead in his tracks. "Ellie?" he asked, as though not believing what he was seeing. We were all wearing shorts and I was pleased to note that we had better legs than they did. Jean had lumpy thighs and thick ankles and Max's legs were skinny and hairy, as usual.

Once out of his perennial jeans, Sam had turned out to have excellent legs, rather like a runner's. Men's legs had never been a turn-on for me, but I found myself looking at his more than once.

As though he had done it a hundred times before, Sam casually draped his arm around my shoulder.

"What're you doing in New Jersey?" Max asked me, sounding accusing.

"I have a share in a house," I said.

"You?" He had the look of a man who had just taken a blow to the gut.

I nodded, refusing to make a big deal of it. After all, normal people took shares all the time. Only cheapskates spent summer weekends in the city if they could afford to get out.

I knew he was dying to ask me where I got the money for a share. As though not really caring, I asked, "What're you guys doing down here?"

"We're staying with friends," said Jean, avoiding my eyes, as well she should. She was the one who should be wishing for a tidal wave.

"You have a share for the whole summer?" Max asked, still not quite believing me.

"With Richard and Alicia," I said. "And another couple who are film editors."

Max's squint deepened into a frown. "I didn't know you stayed in touch with Richard and Alicia."

"I do now," I said.

The consternation on Max's face was beautiful to behold. I'm sure he had been picturing me holed up somewhere praying for him to come back to me. Not that I hadn't been, but at least it wasn't obvious. I mean here I was with another man, wasn't I? And a man with good legs at that.

Now Max was staring at Sam. I saw a glint of recognition in his eyes as though he, too, were seeing the slight resemblance between them. Did he think I had run out and found the first Max clone I could find?

"Oh," I said, "Sam, this is Max and Jean. Sam Wiley."

"Hi," said Jean, in her breathy little poetess voice. Well, okay, so she's got a rather nice voice. It didn't even begin to make up for her lumpy thighs.

Max didn't say anything for a moment. Max just stared. "The documentary filmmaker?" he finally asked, his eyes pleading for me to deny it.

"That's right," said Sam, holding out his hand to Max. "You in the film business, Mac?"

I loved the "Mac" but Max didn't even notice. "Max teaches at NYU," I said, making it sound negligible at best.

"I've taught some of your techniques in my classes," said Max, coming across now as the sycophant he was. "I just saw your latest one at Lincoln Center. I thought it was brilliant."

Brilliant was a word Max used sparingly.

"See, Ellie?" said Sam, pulling me in closer to him with his arm and nuzzling my hair with his nose. "Some people appreciate the army ant."

I could see Max taking in this loving gesture. Max would never have been seen in public doing something like that. Aside from this little bit of revenge, though, I thought it felt good. For a moment I wished it were for real.

"How've you been, Ellie?" asked Jean, looking at me for the first time.

I gave her a look that cut her dead. I looked at her with the kind of loathing I usually reserved for species like army ants and cockroaches.

Max started to stutter. "Maybe we could, uh... Maybe we could all, uh . . ." I had never seen Max at such a loss for words. "Maybe we could, uh, have a drink to—"

I leaned my face to the side so that my cheek rested on Sam's hand. "I don't think so, Max," I said, and had the satisfaction of seeing his face flush with embarrassment. The rat hadn't the slightest interest in me. He just wanted a chance to talk with one of his film idols.

"Nice meeting you, Mac," said Sam, really stressing the *Mac* this time, and a moment later we were continuing on our walk.

I wanted to look back and see if Max was staring after me with longing, but I forced myself not to. Anyway, it was probably Sam he'd be staring after with longing. Max seemed to be quite the little groupie when he was around someone who really made films.

Once out of hearing distance, I gave an exultant laugh. "That was perfect," I said, moving out from under Sam's arm so he could feel free to drop the pretense. I was a little sorry, though, when he let his arm drop to his side.

"He seemed like a nice guy," said Sam.

"I couldn't have planned it better myself. And you know something? I think you were even more effective than Scott would've been."

"Scott? You mean the actor?"

"I had fantasies of running into them when I was with Scott and having Jean drooling with envy. And it wouldn't hurt to have Max see me with a young stud, either."

"Rather than an old stud like me."

"You're not old and you're not a stud," I said, probably too quickly.

"I guess I'll say thanks to half of that," said Sam.

"He was so impressed," I went on. "You're the kind of person who really impresses him. Someone who's independent and out there doing what he would like to be doing."

"Nothing's stopping him," said Sam.

"Fear is stopping him. He's afraid he can't really do it. All he can do is theorize about it."

"You're being too hard on him. Come on, Ellie, all the guy did was have an affair."

"*All?* That's *all* he did? He betrayed my love and my trust and took up with my best friend. She's the one I want to get, though."

Max looked over at me. "Get?"

"Yes. As in 'get revenge.'"

"Would you go back to him?"

"No." After I said it, I suddenly realized that it was the truth. I felt so relieved all of a sudden that I let out a whoop and began to whirl in circles on the sand. I didn't want to go back to him; I really didn't. I had met the enemy and come out of the encounter with my pride intact. Up until then my deepest fear was that I'd end up crawling back to Max.

When I finally stopped, Sam was standing watching me with a smile. "Did you mean that?"

"I did. I really did."

"You're just feeling euphoric that you won the first encounter."

"I don't think so, I really don't. I hardly know you, Sam, but I'm happier walking along the beach with you than I would be if Max had told Jean to buzz off and tried to get me to go back to him. I mean, that would have been nice, but I wouldn't have gone and it wouldn't have made me happy."

Sam's smile turned a little doubtful. "You couldn't be over him this soon."

"I still have feelings for Max. I can't help it; we were married a long time. But I don't want him back."

"Then what's the point of getting revenge?"

"The point is it would make me feel good."

"I think you'd feel a lot better if you just got on with your life."

He was wrong, though. If I was feeling this good just over a chance encounter, I was sure I'd feel ten times as good if I got some real revenge. I wanted Max crawling to me on his knees, tears in his eyes over what he lost. I wanted Jean begging me for forgiveness, having come to the realization too late that friendship was worth a dozen men. I wanted it all and I wanted to be able to savor it.

I grabbed him by the hand and started to run down the beach. When I finally stopped to catch my breath, I said, "You know something, Sam?"

"What's that?"

"I like you better right now than I ever liked Max."

"Does this mean—"

"It means that I never really liked Max. We were never friends. Sure, I loved him, and sure, I was under his spell, but I never actually liked him."

"How do you love someone you don't like?"

"It's easy," I said.

"It would be impossible for me."

"I think it happens all the time. You're sexually attracted to someone and you mistake it for love, but you don't have to like the person."

"But you said *mistake* it for love. That isn't love."

"Okay, what's love, then?"

He stood for a minute giving it some thought. "For me it's a person who's more interesting to be around than any other person. Someone who my mind reaches out to, and my body and my soul."

"That wouldn't happen overnight."

"That kind doesn't. If it's there at all, though, you get little hints of it."

I was really getting caught up in his vision of love. "What kind of little hints?"

He looked down at me, his eyes gleaming. "Do you know what I'd like to do right now more than anything else in the world?"

Oh, no, I thought, *he's going to get romantic; it's much too soon.* "What?" I asked, hoping I was wrong.

"I'd like to bury you up to the neck in sand."

I grinned at him. "You know what, Sam? Because I like you, I'm going to let you."

I think it was the most fun I'd ever had with a man.

I SLEPT THAT NIGHT for the first time in weeks. I hadn't expected to when I climbed up into the top bunk and Sam climbed into the bottom. I expected to be awake all night again, and I knew I couldn't drag the TV into the room and expect Sam to be able to sleep. I hadn't even had a drink, or at least not since right after dinner. But for some reason I didn't want those aids to sleep. I think what I wanted was to savor that encounter on the beach, over and over, much as I had savored my fantasies of revenge. The thing about the beach was, it was real. I was ready to stay awake all night and, what's more, I expected to enjoy it.

And yet I slept straight through. If a little bit of revenge could give me a good night's sleep, I tried to imagine what a lot of revenge might do for me.

I couldn't wait to find out.

The more
you love romance ...
the more
you'll love this offer

Mail this heart today! (See inside)

**Join us on a Harlequin Honeymoon
and we'll give you
4 free books
A free bracelet watch
And a free mystery gift**

154 CIH NBH8 (U-H-A-10/89)

IT'S A
HARLEQUIN HONEYMOON—
A SWEETHEART
OF A FREE OFFER!
HERE'S WHAT YOU GET:

1. **Four New Harlequin American Romance® Novels—FREE!**
   Take a Harlequin Honeymoon with your four exciting romances—yours FREE from Harlequin Reader Service®. Each of these hot-off-the-press novels brings you the passion and tenderness of today's greatest love stories . . . your free passports to bright new worlds of love and foreign adventure.

2. **A Lovely Bracelet Watch—FREE!**
   You'll love your elegant bracelet watch—this classic LCD quartz watch is a perfect expression of your style and good taste—and it is yours FREE as an added thanks for giving our Reader Service a try.

3. **An Exciting Mystery Bonus—FREE!**
   You'll be thrilled with this surprise gift. It is elegant as well as practical.

4. **Money-Saving Home Delivery!**
   Join Harlequin Reader Service® and enjoy the convenience of previewing four new books every month delivered right to your home. Each book is yours for only $2.74*—21¢ less per book than the cover price. And there is *no* extra charge for postage and handling. Great savings plus total convenience add up to a sweetheart of a deal for you! If you're not completely satisfied, you may cancel at any time, for any reason, simply by sending us a note or shipping statement marked ''cancel'' or by returning any shipment to us at our cost.

5. **Free Insiders' Newsletter**
   It's *heart to heart*®, the indispensible insiders' look at our most popular writers, upcoming books, even comments from readers and much more.

6. **More Surprise Gifts**
   Because our home subscribers are our most valued readers, when you join the Harlequin Reader Service®, we'll be sending you additional free gifts from time to time—as a token of our appreciation.

START YOUR HARLEQUIN HONEYMOON TODAY—JUST
COMPLETE, DETACH AND MAIL YOUR FREE-OFFER CARD

Get your fabulous gifts
ABSOLUTELY FREE!

MAIL THIS CARD TODAY.

PLACE
FREE!

GIVE YOUR HEART
TO HARLEQUIN

YES! Please send me my four Harlequin American Romance®
novels FREE, along with my free bracelet watch and free
mystery gift. I wish to receive all the benefits of the Harlequin
Reader Service® as explained on the opposite page.

NAME _____
(PLEASE PRINT)

ADDRESS _____ APT. _____

CITY _____ STATE _____

ZIP CODE _____

154 CIH NBH8 (U-H-A-10/89)

OFFER LIMITED TO ONE PER HOUSEHOLD AND NOT VALID TO CURRENT
HARLEQUIN AMERICAN ROMANCE® SUBSCRIBERS.

HARLEQUIN READER SERVICE® "NO RISK" GUARANTEE
—There's no obligation to buy—and the free books and gifts remain yours to keep.
—You pay the low members-only discount price and receive books before they appear in stores.
—You may end your subscription anytime by sending us a note or shipping statement marked
"cancel", or by returning any shipment to us at our cost.

PRINTED IN U.S.A.
© 1989 HARLEQUIN ENTERPRISES LIMITED

154 CIH NBH8 (U-H-A-10/89)

START YOUR
HARLEQUIN HONEYMOON TODAY.
JUST COMPLETE, DETACH AND MAIL YOUR
FREE OFFER CARD.

If offer card is missing, write to: Harlequin Reader Service® 901 Fuhrmann Blvd
P.O. Box 1867 Buffalo NY 14269-1867

DETACH AND MAIL TODAY!

BUSINESS REPLY CARD

FIRST CLASS MAIL   PERMIT NO. 717   BUFFALO, NY

POSTAGE WILL BE PAID BY ADDRESSEE

HARLEQUIN READER SERVICE
901 FUHRMANN BLVD
PO BOX 1867
BUFFALO NY 14240-9952

NO POSTAGE
NECESSARY
IF MAILED
IN THE
UNITED STATES

Chapter Eight

Review/FILM
ROBOT LOVER
by Ellie Thomas

In this fine new film from director Nick Bly, a young married woman (played hauntingly by the gifted Meryl Sleepover) has an affair with the robot that they purchased to tutor their mentally disturbed son. William Curt once again astonishes us with his subtle performance as the robot. Shelley Hinters, in a cameo role as the mother-in-law, is alone worth the seven-dollar admission. This is a movie that is sure to have people lining up around the block and has my vote for best movie of the year.

Rated X

"HEY, ELLIE, I gotta talk to you," yelled Woody from his breezy office.

I walked in and took a seat, giving him my sunniest smile. And why not? I had now slept soundly for three nights in a row and was feeling terrific. Revenge, as an obsession, appeared to be losing its control over me. I'd still like to get Max and Jean, but I guess not enough to lose sleep over.

"I hate to keep complaining about your reviews," Woody said, eyeing me a little nervously.

"Then don't."

"But on your recommendation, I took my wife to see *Varsity Werewolves* over the weekend."

"Didn't you love it?" I asked him, a false note of enthusiasm in my voice.

"Kathy threw up in the movie."

"*In* the theater?"

"She made it to the ladies' room."

"What about you?"

Woody rolled his eyes. "I thought it was pure garbage."

"I really loved that movie."

"For God's sake, Ellie, the werewolves ate the opposing team's quarterback. I don't think I've ever seen so much blood and guts on a movie screen."

"I don't remember that."

"You don't *remember* it? How could you not remember it? That was the climax of the movie. I don't think I'll forget that scene as long as I live. There were kids in that movie theater who will probably have nightmares for the rest of their lives as a result of that scene."

"It was a pretty memorable movie."

"It was deplorable! It was the most tasteless movie I've ever seen. It was filthy and disgusting and gross."

"You wanted me to be more positive in my reviews, Woody."

"I don't see how you could've sat through that movie and then written that review."

It was easy. I sat through it asleep and made notes of the remarks I overheard from the other people walking out of the screening.

"It's beyond me how it even got released," said Woody.

"The football sequences were . . ." An adjective didn't come to mind.

"You know what, Ellie?"

"You're firing me."

"No, I'm not firing you. I'm having a talk with you. But the scuttlebutt is that your reviews bear very little relationship to the movies you're reviewing."

"First you complained because I didn't like the movies, now you're complaining because I like them."

"That's not what I'm saying."

"I can't seem to please you."

"Ellie, difficult as it may be to believe, there are actually some people in New York who go to a movie or stay away from a movie on your say-so alone. You're confusing those people. What's more, you're doing them a disservice."

I tried to look properly chastised. It wasn't difficult as I knew he was right. "I'll do better, Woody, I promise."

"You need some time off, Ellie?"

"No, Woody. Thanks anyway."

"You need a shoulder to cry on?"

"I'm not crying anymore."

Woody's face showed instant relief. "Great. Good to hear that. Listen, you want two tickets to U2 Saturday night?"

"Are you kidding? I'd kill for two tickets to U2."

He reached into his pocket and brought out a small envelope, handing it to me. "Be my guest," he said.

I opened the envelope to make sure he wasn't joking, and it did indeed hold the tickets. "For this, I'm your slave forever," I told him.

"What are you viewing today?"

"*Exterminator.*"

"That old Schwarzenegger movie? What're you seeing that for?"

"Not *The Exterminator*, just *Exterminator*. This one is about your friendly, neighborhood bug killer."

"Well, enjoy," said Woody, sounding doubtful.

I HAD A COUPLE of hours to kill before the screening and I spent them riding uptown and back several times on the Seventh Avenue subway. By the third time the train pulled into the Columbus Circle station, all the panhandler regulars knew me and stopped hitting me up for money. I felt energized by the speed and the air-conditioning and the people.

After wasting two hours, I got to the screening a little late and just had time to sit down next to Roy Campbell, one of the reviewers for the *Voice*, before the lights went down.

"How're you doin', Thomas?" Roy asked me.

"Great," I said.

"You stayin' awake for this one?"

I tried to look affronted.

"Hey, don't give me that look. I've heard your snores clear in the back."

"I'm staying awake for this one," I told him.

One of the guys in front of us turned around and said to Roy, "I've got five dollars that says she'll be asleep before the opening credits have rolled."

"You're on," said Roy.

I slid down in my seat and rested my head. This move brought a groan from Roy. "I'm not tired, I swear," I said to him.

I stayed awake through the entire movie. Five minutes into it, I was wishing I was back riding the subway. It was garbage, pure garbage. Plus there were countless close-ups of cockroaches, not my favorite insect. Although if I had to name my favorite insect it would take me a while to come up with one.

Halfway through the two-hour movie I realized that I enjoyed sleeping more than I enjoyed watching horror films. If a genie had appeared at the moment and asked me for my fondest wish, it would've been never to have to see another one.

Afterward Roy took me to lunch with the five dollars I had won for him. As we sat in Burger King, he asked, "How are you gonna review something that bad?"

"I'm going to redo it," I told him.

"What're you talkin' about?"

"I'm going to write the review of the movie I would have made of it. I'm going to rewrite it, redirect it and turn it into an instant classic."

"I can't wait to read this," said Roy.

I found I couldn't wait to write it. It would be the first time I'd used any creativity in years.

SAM KNOCKED at my door at eight o'clock that night. "What're you doing?" he asked when I opened it.

"Smoking and watching a movie."

"I didn't think we were allowed to smoke in here," he said.

"I have a floor fan that blows the smoke to my window exhaust fan that blows it out. I also have an air purifier."

"Can I come in?"

I stood aside and he entered my room. He lit a cigarette and looked over at the TV set. "What're you watching?"

"*Reds*. It's one of my favorite movies. I'm only going to watch the first two hours tonight."

"Can I watch it with you?"

"Sure."

I opened up the futon couch so that we could stretch our legs out, and then set the large bowl of popcorn I had made between us. Sam must have finally unpacked because he was wearing a pair of khaki pants instead of his usual jeans, and a white T-shirt with a picture of a green and red parrot on it. Under the parrot it said Amazon Camp.

Sam kicked off his shoes, made himself comfortable and reached for a handful of popcorn. I had only watched a few minutes of the movie so I rewound it and started it over again. The first part, with the witnesses, is my favorite, anyway.

We watched the first half hour in silence broken only by the crunching of popcorn. I was just thinking that he was a good person to watch a movie with because he didn't talk while he watched it when he said, "It doesn't seem the same. I remember at the time I saw it thinking that I'd like to see it again, but it seems different this time."

"Not the witnesses."

"No, they seem the same, but the rest doesn't."

I put the VCR on pause and turned to face him. "You know what I think it is?"

"Probably our failing memories."

"No. I remember it perfectly, I saw it at least seven times. It's the small screen."

"I think you're right."

"I *am* right. Put a good movie on a small screen and it makes it seem like television."

Sam nodded. "Like watching a movie on an airplane. I never like in-flight movies."

"That's probably because you get drunk when you fly."

"I can enjoy a movie when I'm drinking. No, the small screen does something to it."

"It diminishes it. It's an epic, but you lose that and you also lose most of the good camera shots. You even lose some of the people in some of the scenes."

"It makes it boring."

"Yes," I agreed. "It becomes like television."

"I'm glad my movies aren't on video."

"You *wish* they were."

"Okay, the money would be nice."

"The money would be great."

"You're right. I wouldn't have to keep getting funding."

I picked up the remote control—which, like my father, I had come to love—and flicked off the movie.

Sam said, "I don't mind watching the rest. It's worth it to be able to smoke indoors."

"You can stay."

"Thanks."

"You know something, Sam? I hate to admit it but Max was right."

"No one's wrong all the time."

"I mean about television. He would never allow one in the apartment and I'm beginning to see why."

"The news is good on TV."

"Yes."

"And sports."

"But that's all."

"Channel Thirteen gets some good documentaries."

"That's what I hear."

"They had one on the Amazon."

"I didn't have a TV when that was on."

Sam lit another cigarette. "So, you want to go out?"

"No. I feel like staying home. Unless you feel like going for a subway ride."

"No, thanks," said Sam. "Want to go to a movie this weekend?"

"Are you busy Saturday night?" I asked him, remembering my U2 tickets.

"You going to the shore again?"

"That's every other weekend."

"I'm not busy."

"I don't want to interfere with you and Philippa."

"We're not dating."

"Why not?"

"Are you hinting that you'd like me to date Philippa?"

"No. I just don't want to monopolize you, that's all."

"I don't mind being monopolized."

"Good. Then what're you doing Saturday night?"

"What would you like to do?"

"I've got tickets to U2 Saturday night. They're playing at the Garden. Anyway, you're welcome to go with me."

"You're asking me out for Saturday night? That's great, Ellie. I hate to be sitting home alone on date night."

"It's so embarrassing," I said, getting into it.

"You're stuck with watching TV with your parents."

"Or taking your little brother to the movies and hoping you don't see anyone you know."

"Anyway, you just saved my life. We'll go out together Saturday night and no one will know we don't have dates."

"We'll maintain our reputations."

"And maybe even have a good time."

"At U2? We'll have a great time!"

"U2. Is that a rock concert?"

I nodded, wondering where he'd been. I guess they hadn't heard of U2 on the Amazon.

"I'm a little old to be going to a rock concert."

"Nonsense. You're never too old."

"I'm not even sure I know who they are."

"You'll recognize the music."

"Is it hard rock?"

"It's good, old-fashioned rock and roll."

Sam gave a casual shrug. "Yeah, okay."

"No, Sam," I said. "You have to show a little more enthusiasm than that. All over the city people are killing for tickets to U2. I could probably scalp these outside the Garden for a couple of hundred bucks each."

"Okay, I'd like to go."

"I said *enthusiasm*."

Sam grinned. "*Wow!* Far out. Tickets to U2. Out of sight!"

I dumped the bowl of popcorn over his head, and in retaliation he grabbed me in a head lock and pushed my nose into the popcorn all over his chest. It was rather like wrestling with my brother when I was a kid, so I reached out and started to tickle him. That made him let go of me and we both started laughing. If I'd ever dumped popcorn on Max, he would have made me wash the sheets and then killed me. Somehow, though, Max wasn't the type you dumped popcorn on.

"This U2 concert," said Sam.

"Yes?"

"Does this mean we have to get stoned?" he asked, picking popcorn out of his hair and beard.

"This is U2, not the Grateful Dead."

"Good, 'cause I don't like the looks of our neighborhood drug dealer."

"You know who he is?"

"I know who one of them is. I think that building directly across from ours is a crack house."

"I would've thought they'd move it when they saw that banner going up."

"Hell, that's good advertising. Now people know exactly where to come." He got off the couch and cleaned up the rest of the popcorn, putting it back in the bowl and then eating it. He said, "Philippa's forming a neighborhood group against crack. They're going to hold a sit-in Friday night."

"Are you participating?" I asked him.

"Sure. Aren't you? This is too nice a block to have this happen to it. Every time I'm on the street someone tries to buy from me. I think maybe I ought to get a new pair of jeans."

"It's not your jeans," I said. "Pot dealers might wear torn jeans, but crack dealers wear trendy clothes and lots of gold jewelry."

"Are you saying my clothes are out of style."

"Yes."

"Good. I'd hate you to think of me as a trendy guy."

"Don't worry, Sam, no one's going to think that. So what's this sit-in?"

"What we're going to do is, everyone's going to take a chair outside and sit around on the sidewalk. The main thing is just to be visible, but when the cars start pulling up and stopping, we're going to write down their license numbers."

"And do what with them?"

Sam shrugged. "We just thought it might make the buyers nervous. And when it gets dark, we're going to shine flashlights on their cars, kind of put them in the spotlight. So, are you going to join us?"

"I'd like to," I said. I had nothing better to do on Friday night and I liked the idea of giving the crack dealers a hard time.

"Good."

"But what happens when they open fire on us?"

"Then we call the police." Sam got up and walked to the window. "Come here, look at this."

I joined him at the window and looked out. Down in the street three late-model cars were double-parked in front of the building across the street. Business seemed to be booming.

The phone rang and I jumped. I stared at it as it rang twice more, then I picked it up.

"Hi, Ellie." It was Max.

"Hello, Max," I said, looking over at Sam. He was still staring out the window but I saw his back tense up. With me, it was my stomach that was tensing up.

"How are things going?"

"What things, Max?"

"Everything. Are you doing all right?"

"I've got a roof over my head, if that's what you mean. I don't have air-conditioning. I don't have a real bed. I don't have my own kitchen and my own bathroom. But I do have a nineteen-inch Sony Trinitron and a VCR. I was just watching *Reds*."

"Do you have to be so bitter, Ellie?"

"Bitter? Don't make me laugh. What do I have to be bitter about?"

"This doesn't sound like you."

"I've changed."

"Is Sam with you?"

"Sam? You mean Sam Wiley? As a matter of fact, at the moment he's standing at the window watching the crack house across the street."

"Nobody told you to move into a tenement."

"I'm not in a tenement. I'm in a very good building in a very good neighborhood on the Upper West Side."

"Look, I'll call you when you're in a better mood."

"What did you want, Max?"

"I just wanted to talk."

"About what?"

I saw Sam turn around, wink at me and then head for the door. "Hold on a minute," I said to Max, and then put my hand over the mouthpiece. "You don't have to leave," I told him.

"You need some privacy," he said, going out the door and closing it softly behind him.

"Sam's gone, what did you want to talk about?"

"Where'd you meet him?"

"Not that it's any of your business, but I met him at one of Alicia and Richard's parties."

There was a long pause. I figured Max was trying to think of something insulting to say about Sam, but he admired him too much to insult him. Instead, he surprised me by saying, "I miss you, Ellie."

Something started to twist in my stomach. "When did that start, when you saw me with Sam?"

"No. I missed you before that. Seven years is a long time. I got used to having you around."

I wondered if he missed his bathrobe. Or the ironing board. I didn't think he'd replaced them the way he'd replaced me.

"I keep thinking of all the good times we had," he said, lowering his voice into what he considered his sexy mode. I had always thought of it as sexy, too. He always lowered his voice when sex was imminent and I usually reacted like Pavlov's dog. Funny, but it wasn't affecting me like that this time, perhaps because he wasn't here in person.

"Do you, Max? I keep thinking of the horrible spring you put me through. I always used to love spring."

"Do you remember the time we were on the lake in Central Park and it started to rain?"

Of course I remembered it. At the time I had been madly in love with him and thought he was a wonderful person. And it had ended in our making love for the first time. Not, I might add, on the lake.

I pushed the memory back into my subconscious. "Max, did you call for a walk down memory lane or did you want something?"

There was a silence. I knew that in person Max was now looking hurt. Only his hurt look wasn't going to have any effect on me over the phone. I waited it out.

"I'd like to see you, Ellie," Max said, his sexy voice now changed.

"What for?"

"I'd just like to get together, talk, maybe have dinner somewhere."

"Why?"

"Why? Because I miss you."

"No apologies, Max?"

"It wasn't easy on me, either, you know. I'm not very good at lying and cheating. I was a nervous wreck all spring. I've never been so confused in my life, Ellie."

"Oh? You didn't look particularly confused the day I walked in on you."

"You want to know how I felt that day? I barely made it to the bathroom in time to throw up. That's how I felt."

"Did Jean hold your head?"

"Okay, I can understand your wanting to get back at me. I deserve it. I admit that. I went crazy last spring and I don't understand it and you'll never know how much I wish it hadn't happened."

I felt myself beginning to soften. This was my husband I was talking to, the man I had loved ever since college. He probably knew me better than anyone had ever known me. Maybe our marriage could survive an affair. If it could, wasn't it worth giving it a try? Wasn't it better than one room and a shared bath in a crack neighborhood?

"How about having dinner with me tomorrow night, Ellie," he was saying, and I thought he sounded a little bit desperate.

"Well..." I said, hoping to hear a little more desperation from him.

"Please. We can go anywhere you like. We can go to Bentley's," he said, naming my favorite restaurant, which he was usually too cheap to take me to. I guessed that was as much desperation as I was going to get from Max.

I took the time to light a cigarette, knowing he'd hear it over the phone and would be forced, by circumstances, to stifle his usual comments. "All right," I agreed, but let some reluctance show in my voice so that he wouldn't think I was a total pushover.

"Great," said Max. And then I heard a voice in the background and the sound of his hand covering the mouthpiece. Anyone else, I would have assumed the voice was from the TV.

"Who was that?" I asked. I had to ask it a couple of more times before he spoke.

"Jean wanted to know who I was talking to."

"*Jean?* Jean's there?"

"She just walked in."

"She's still living there?"

"What's the difference?"

"What do you mean, what's the difference? You want to continue to live with Jean and see me on the side, is that it?"

"Just for a while, Ellie. I'm still confused."

"Too bad," I said, "but I'm not!" And with that I slammed down the phone, hoping it was hard enough to break his ear drum. I unplugged the phone in case he called back, which would be just like Max, and then I left my room and walked down the hall and knocked on Sam's door.

He opened the door and I practically hurled myself inside. In fact I hurled myself right into him and then put my arms around him.

"What's this?"

"Hold me, Sam."

"What did the bastard do to you now?"

"I don't want to talk about him. I just want to be with you."

Sam tried to take a step back, but I hung on.

"Let's go to the kitchen and I'll make you a cup of cocoa," he said, smoothing my hair with one hand and patting me on the back with the other.

"Quit treating me like a child!"

"Come on, Ellie, we'll talk about it."

"I don't want to talk."

"What *do* you want?"

"Make love to me, Sam," I mumbled, finding it difficult to get the words out. I had never before made the first move with a man.

"Sorry, Ellie."

"Please."

"What do you want to do, have an affair with me to get back at Max?"

"It would make it feel more equitable." But that wasn't it, not really. I was feeling rejected again and I greatly needed to feel desirable.

"Not for me. I would feel used."

I pushed him away from me. "Well, that's great. That really makes me feel terrific. First my husband rejects me and now you do."

"If you wanted me I'd be rejecting you, but you don't want me. You just want revenge on Max. Ask me some time when you really want me."

"Why are you so damned reasonable, Sam?"

"I don't know. I'll probably be sorry in the morning."

"I doubt it."

He smiled at that. "Ellie, you barely know me. We haven't even been to a rock concert together yet. Anyway, a moment that intimate should mean something more than wanting revenge on someone else. Or even to feel wanted."

I looked around his room for the first time. He didn't even have a bed. Instead, he had a hammock strung across the corner of the room. Other than that, all there was were several canvas bags. One of the bags was open and I could see clothing inside.

"You sleep in that?" I asked him, looking at the hammock.

"Not conducive to making love," he said.

"Well, if that's all that's stopping you, we could go to my room." But I wasn't serious anymore. He was there for me as a friend, and that was a lot more important than taking my revenge out on Max. "Why a hammock?"

He shrugged. "I got used to it. I carry it with me, which makes renting unfurnished places easy."

I saw something then that I hadn't seen before; Sam was a transient in New York and was probably going to be a transient in my life. Anyone who carried a hammock around with him wasn't looking for a long-term relationship, even if I *had* been inclined in that direction. He was a wanderer, and wanderers didn't put down roots.

"Hey, Sam, I'll take that cup of cocoa."

"And a little sympathy?"

"I'll take anything you want to offer."

"I've got a better idea," said Sam. "Let's go for a walk and I'll buy you ice cream."

For a transient, he sure knew the way to my heart.

Chapter Nine

Review/FILM
EXTERMINATOR
by Ellie Thomas

What happens when you call the exterminator to come out and take care of your roach problem, and instead you get a lunatic in your apartment who is waging a private war, complete with nukes, to rid the city of cockroaches? In this deftly directed comedy, director Howard Ronn once again proves that directing TV commercials is a firm basis for moving up to feature films. Dustin Kaufman plays the role of the exterminator with the kind of masterly depth that proves beyond a doubt that he is America's finest actor. One is moved to laughter in the scene where the exterminator unwittingly blows up an entire block in Soho, only to find out the roaches escaped in time. This is the kind of movie that you're going to want to run out and buy as soon as it comes out in video.

Rated R

I JOINED the neighborhood drug sit-in on Friday night. Philippa had organized it and quite a few people showed up. I had assumed most of the neighborhood departed for the Hamptons or elsewhere for the weekend, but there was a large crowd. Perhaps it had something to do with the fact that most of the beaches were closed due to sewage having been dumped off-shore.

It was almost like a block party. Everyone brought out a folding chair and a thermos of something to drink, and some people were eating their suppers outdoors. There were no children around; either because they didn't think it safe for children to be there or because there weren't any children on our block.

Sam was seated next to Philippa when I joined them, but Philippa wasn't sitting much. Instead she was going around and talking to everyone. She seemed to personally know most of the people living in the neighborhood. She was dressed in a full purple skirt and a low-cut pink top and she looked gypsylike and pretty and most of the men were flirting with her. I was in shorts and a T-shirt and looked just regular. A couple of the men looked at me, but the looks didn't show much depth and none of them talked to me.

There were a couple of possible dealers sitting on the stoop directly across the street, and next to them on the stoop was a gigantic radio playing rap music. They were young and black and they flashed their smiles at us every so often. They were dressed alike in black pants and black T-shirts, and the gold around their necks and on their fingers seemed to set off sparks when it caught the light from the sun setting in the west. They seemed to be observing us with amusement. Maybe they thought it was a party and would come over and try to sell us something. I had no idea what we were supposed to do if that happened, other than say, "No thank you," which is what I always said to street dealers. I always felt stupid being so polite to them when they were asking me to break the law, but I couldn't seem to help it.

"They're just kids," said Sam, seeing me observe them.

"Very rich kids, from the look of all that jewelry," I said.

A car came down the street and slowed down. Philippa yelled to someone, "Take down the number of the license plate." One of our men stepped out into the street and took the number down as one of the men on the stoop stood up and approached the car. We didn't seem to be scaring the dealers, but the man in the car pulled off so fast he burnt rubber. The dealer watched the car take off, and then turned to us, nodded and sat back down on the stoop.

"We're going to get them mad at us if we keep doing that," I said to Sam.

"I think that's the point."

"The point is, how mad do we want to get them?"

"If they try anything, we call the cops."

"Try anything? Like maybe shoot us?"

"Something like that," said Sam, clearly enjoying himself. Perhaps he liked to live dangerously, which would explain his proclivity for jungly places.

"She looks good, doesn't she?" I asked him, nodding my head in the direction of Philippa. She was standing at the curb, her arms folded, staring at the men across the street.

"She's a good-looking woman," said Sam.

He didn't add, "But not as good-looking as you," which was, of course, what I wanted to hear. In an ideal world, men would instantly be attracted to women because of their minds, but in my experience the world was far from ideal. And since it wasn't ideal, I wanted Sam to like my looks.

"You two would look good together," I said, not being able to leave the subject alone.

"Sure we would," said Sam. "She looks rather like my sister."

I instantly cheered up. If I wasn't attracted to men who looked like my brothers, maybe Sam wasn't attracted to women who looked like his sister. On the other hand, maybe he was.

"Are you interested in her?" I asked, hating myself for not being able to drop it. Not that I considered it a crime to want to know where I stood with him.

"You mean as a person or as a woman?"

"You know what I mean," I said, getting annoyed.

"No."

I took another look at Philippa. I would think she'd be interesting to any man. "Why not?"

"Oh, there are several reasons."

"Just give me one."

I, of course, was hinting for him to say it was me he was interested in, since I had decided that I might be interested in him. Sam, however, wasn't falling for that.

"I don't see any point in starting something when I won't be around long enough to finish it."

"Are you saying you won't be in the city long enough to get involved with someone?"

"I'm never around *anywhere* long enough."

"You mean you don't ever have a woman?"

"It's difficult, Ellie. Saying good-bye is very difficult for me. I don't want to have to go through that again."

I supposed that meant that he considered me safe. And I guess I was, hung up on Max the way I was. Or at least the way Sam thought I was hung up on revenge, which I wasn't so much anymore. But I didn't see how he could control his emotions that easily. I didn't want him to be able to control his emotions that easily. I think what I wanted was for him to fall madly, passionately, hopelessly in love with me so that I'd get over feeling rejected by men.

"Don't you ever want to settle down in one place?" I asked him.

"I guess not, or I would have by now. I'm forty-four and I'm happy doing what I'm doing."

"Can you really control your emotions that well?"

"What do you mean?"

"Well, for one thing, Sam, do you ever fall in love unless you know you're going to be somewhere long enough?"

"No. You can't help falling in love. If I knew I was going to be leaving, though, I wouldn't do anything about it."

"You mean you could fall in love with someone and then just leave?"

"I don't think you understand how important my work is to me."

"I guess your wife understood," I said, which wasn't very nice and I regretted it as soon as I saw his face.

"Yes, she did."

"I'm sorry."

"That's all right. I loved her. She just didn't understand that I needed more than just her. I needed my work equally as much. She viewed my films as competition."

I didn't tell him that I could understand that attitude. Women were quite capable of revolving their lives around a man and it was maddening when men wouldn't do the same.

"What kind of work did she do?"

"Nothing she was really interested in, which was the problem."

I felt very smug knowing that I had a career, until I remembered that I didn't care very much for reviewing lousy films.

I had been so busy watching Sam's reactions that I hadn't seen what was going on. I was aware of a buzz around me and looked across the street in time to see several scary-looking men coming out of the building across the street. It looked as though the dealers controlled the entire building.

"There's going to be trouble," said Sam. "Be careful." Before I knew what was happening, he got up and went into our building.

Philippa came over and asked, "Did Sam go inside?"

"Yes, I don't understand it," I said, surprised that he would be the first one to run.

"He'll be back. We've got it all planned out," said Philippa, a mysterious look on her face.

Another car pulled up across the street, and this time the dealers surrounded it and no one had the guts to run out to get the license number.

All of a sudden the front first-floor window in our building was opened and a spotlight was trained on the street.

Then Sam came out of the door, a movie camera on his shoulder. When he started filming the action across the street, they all started shielding their faces and heading back into the house. A spontaneous cheer went up from our side of the street.

Sam sat down next to me and set the camera carefully on the sidewalk.

"What are you going to do with the film?" I asked him. "Show it to the cops?"

"What film?"

"The film you just shot."

"Do you have any idea how much film costs, Ellie?"

"You mean you were faking it?"

"It worked, didn't it?"

It also worked on the cars that slowed down after that. As soon as the driver would spot Sam with the camera, he'd leave in a hurry.

Philippa came by, a big smile on her face. "Good work," she said to Sam.

"They'll just come out again when we go to bed," I pointed out.

"We're not going to bed," said Philippa. "We're going to take shifts staying up all night."

Great timing, I thought, *just when I was finally over my insomnia.*

I HAD TAKEN the two-to-four shift with Sam and slept until noon the next day. I got my laundry together and carried it to the laundromat on Amsterdam, then had breakfast in a coffee shop while I waited for it. I bought a *Times* and carried it back to the laundromat to read while my laundry dried.

It was about ninety degrees and humid outside. The inside of the laundromat was hotter, and along with the smell of bleach, made me feel sick. I stood outside the door and read the paper. There were fires all over the west and one in Yellowstone Park. I remembered the fires in the mountains when I was a kid. Sometimes the smoke would come all the way to where we lived and make it dark out in the middle of the day. We might get a lot of things in Manhattan, but at least we didn't get forest fires. Or earthquakes. Although I'd settle for a small earthquake if it would only cool off the weather.

Sam was sitting on the stoop when I got back with my laundry.

"What're you doing this afternoon?" he asked me.

"I'm going to the park."

"How about an air-conditioned movie?"

The last thing I felt like doing was sitting through another movie, even if it was cool inside. "If you want to cool off," I said, "come with me. Just watching the polar bears always cools me off."

"Polar bears?"

"The new zoo is open. You'll love it; it's really nice."

I usually just went over to see the polar bears, but Sam insisted on seeing all of it. He got really excited about a display of leaf ants and it was all I could do to drag him away from it.

The polar bear was up to his usual. There was a thick Plexiglass partition between him and the spectators, and the polar bear would throw himself against it, coming up out of the water with enough force to shake the transparent wall. Little children would scream, and the polar bear would dive back into the water, swim the length again, and then throw himself against the wall once more. I never got tired of watching him and he never seemed to tire of his attacks.

"Don't you love him?" I asked Sam. I was just crazy about that polar bear.

"I feel sorry for him."

"What do you mean? He's having a great time."

"He shouldn't be penned in like that."

"You should've seen the zoo before; it was disgusting. But I think they've done really well by the animals this time."

"It's not the same as being free."

"Come on, that bear's enjoying himself."

"You think that trying to attack food and coming up against a hard, invisible wall is enjoyable?"

"I think he's having fun."

"I think he's frustrated."

"I take it you don't approve of zoos."

"Of course I don't approve of zoos," said Sam. "No one who loves animals could approve of zoos."

"I haven't noticed that you're a vegetarian."

"You haven't seen me eat meat."

"You mean you are?"

"If at all possible. Unless I'm stuck in the middle of the jungle somewhere and the only thing to eat is fish or wild boar."

"I'll bet you wear leather shoes."

He looked down at his running shoes. I looked to see if he was wearing a leather belt, but he wasn't.

"I admire you," I said.

"It's just something I feel strongly about."

"I love animals, and occasionally I think I ought to stop eating them, but I really crave red meat. I'm a carnivore."

"Do you have a fur coat?" he asked me, and he didn't sound in the least censorious.

"No, and I wouldn't. But I do have a leather bomber jacket," I admitted. Wanting to get off the subject, I said, "Why don't you do a film on polar bears?" I wondered what he would liken them to.

"They're not endangered."

"Neither are ants," I said. "Everywhere you go there's ants. I could personally step on a million ants this summer and there still wouldn't be a shortage."

"The rain forest is endangered, and all its species. That's what interests me."

"How about whales?"

"I like whales," said Sam, "but I'm concentrating on the Amazon region. There are enough things there to keep me occupied the rest of my life."

"The rest of your *life*?"

"Yes."

"You're not going to ever retire?"

"Not if I can help it."

"You must really like it down there."

"I love it."

I tried to remember what it was like in *The Emerald Forest*. "Isn't it hot?"

"Compared to New York? No."

"It's not usually this hot here."

"With the hole in the ozone layer, it might very well be from now on."

"Are you one of those people who worry about the ozone layer?" I asked.

"Everyone should worry about it," said Sam. "It's our world and it's the only one we have."

"Does your making documentaries change anything?"

"I hope so. If I didn't think so, I wouldn't do it."

I turned to him and put my arms around him, giving him a big bear hug.

"What was that for?" asked Sam, but he didn't pull away.

"Just to thank you."

"For what?"

"For being such a nice person. For caring about animals and other things. I wish I were exactly like you."

Sam chuckled. "I'm glad you're not."

"You know what I mean."

In reply, his arms went around me and practically lifted me off the ground. It was much too hot out to be wrapped up in each other like that, but I didn't mind and Sam didn't seem to, either. I saw some little children watching us and broke away. But he took my hand and we walked around the rest of the zoo hand in hand.

THE AREA around Madison Square Garden was flooded with people. All the people who hadn't left the city for the weekend seemed to be converging on the U2 concert. There were people selling U2 T-shirts and people buying and selling concert tickets and a few shoppers carrying Macy's bags who were trying to get through the dense crowd and into Penn Station.

We took the escalator up and found our seats. Sam stood for a moment, surveying the crowd, and then said to me, "I don't know about you, but I'm feeling older by the minute."

"They don't get as young a crowd as some groups."

"Everyone here looks half my age. I'll bet I'm the oldest one in the Garden."

"Buy one of their T-shirts and put it on. It'll take off ten years."

"I'm not sure ten years would do it. Why is it, Ellie, that I feel young in foreign countries, and as soon as I come back here, I'm made to feel old?"

"You're not that old, Sam. You must've grown up on rock music."

"I grew up on it, but I think I've grown past it. Do you really like this group?"

"I love them. You will, too, I promise."

When the concert began, Sam looked as though he was in a state of shock. Admittedly the volume was high, and the acoustics being what they are at the Garden, the bass seemed to seep inside of you and set your body throbbing. Still, he didn't complain until the young women in front of us stood up and started to move in time with the music, totally blocking our view.

I stood up as soon as they did, but it took Sam a little longer. Finally he stood and shouted in my ear, "Doesn't anyone in New York appreciate silence?"

"Not at a rock concert," I shouted back.

I think he said a few more things, but I was no longer paying attention. Instead, I was falling in love with Bono. Along with every other female in the place—and maybe some of the males—I wanted to capture him off the stage and take him home with me. He got to me in a way no actor ever could. Possibly it was because he was being completely himself on the stage, his real, true self in a way an actor never is. I knew with him that if I got him alone he wouldn't stop playing the role because he *was* the role.

At the end Bono made a plea for Amnesty International into the microphone. Like Sam, he had a social conscience, and I thought that added to his appeal. I felt like running up on stage and swearing to Bono that I would give my next year's salary to Amnesty International if he would just come home with me for the night. And it wasn't for revenge, either, because I doubted whether Max even knew who he was.

Sam looked exhausted when the concert was over. For me it had gone by much too quickly. I was still in a daze as we left the cool building and walked out into what felt like one gigantic laundromat.

"Didn't you love them?" I asked Sam, wanting to spend the rest of the night talking about the concert. If I had been with a female friend, I'm sure we would have gone on and on about Bono and The Edge, but I was pretty sure Sam wasn't going to go for that.

"I think I would have liked them better with the volume turned down a bit."

Sam guided me across the street into a bar in one of the hotels. I hardly noticed as we pushed through the crowd around the bar and, moments later, Sam handed me a glass of beer. He drank his down while I was still wondering why I was there.

"They got to you, didn't they?" he finally asked me.

"I'm sorry you didn't enjoy it." I was sorry, but I didn't understand it.

"There were some nice songs and it was fun watching you enjoy it. You certainly know how to move with abandon."

"I couldn't help it. I felt like the music was inside of me."

"Well, yes—it did feel rather like that. I believe I like outdoor concerts better."

"I think I'm in love with Bono."

"The lead singer?"

I nodded.

"Don't ever make the mistake, Ellie, of falling in love with rock stars or documentary filmmakers. It's not conducive to a stable love life."

"I had a stable love life," I said, "and where did it get me? A room in someone else's apartment and a love life that adds up to zero."

Sam said something else, but I wasn't listening. I was fantasizing my life with Bono. I was sure he was the type of person who would take me with him when he was on the road and would include me in all aspects of his life. I'd be the perfect wife for Bono, just as I had been the perfect wife for Max. Only unlike Max, Bono seemed loving and caring. I didn't think he'd ever cheat on me with my best friend. I wouldn't mind living in Ireland, either. At least it wasn't as hot over there.

I felt Sam's arm go around my shoulder and give me a shake. "Are you still with me?" he asked.

"Yeah," I said.

"Do you really fall in love that easily?"

"I guess so."

Sam looked intrigued. "You mean that if I were to get up on stage and start singing, you'd fall in love with me?"

"Can you sing?" I asked him.

"Can't even carry a tune."

"Then I probably wouldn't."

"So you're falling in love with what he is rather than who he is."

"I don't see the distinction."

"Would you want someone to fall in love with you because of your movie reviews?"

"Not the ones I've done lately, no."

"But the others?"

"I think that what you do has to do with who you are," I told him. "Because of the kind of person you are, you're making films about the rain forest. Because of the kind of person Max is, he teaches."

"And because of the kind of person you are, you review movies?"

"It doesn't work in my case," I said.

"Why not?"

"Because I'm not doing what I set out to do."

"Why aren't you?"

"I guess 'cause I got married."

"Then now's your chance."

This wasn't very satisfying at all. I wanted to talk about Bono and he was turning it around on me. "Let's walk

home, Sam,'' I said. I felt like working off some of the
energy I had picked up at the concert.

"Sixty blocks?"

"It's an easy walk."

"Through Times Square? It's a jungle there." He actually sounded nervous about it. To me Times Square was
nothing compared to surviving in the Amazon.

"Then you should feel right at home," I told him.

"Only for you," he said.

I leaned in close to him. "And we can hold hands and
snuggle a little along the way."

"While you pretend I'm Bono?"

"No, while I pretend you're a famous filmmaker
whom I'm about to have a wild, adventurous love affair
with."

"It doesn't all have to be pretend," he said.

And that was the really exciting part, because it didn't.
He might be leaving soon and I might still be getting over
Max, but life still went on and there was the possibility of
anything happening.

Chapter Ten

Review/FILM
SLUMBER PARTY PANIC
by Ellie Thomas

Gather up your kids and take them to this delight-ful romp. And if you don't have any kids, borrow some. What do you get when you pit the most pop-ular clique in junior high against a mass murderer who is on the loose? You get Sam Goatherd's tour de force, *Slumber Party Panic*. In the tradition of Monty Python, the director has us screaming with laughter as one by one the mass murderer (Clint Westwood) tortures and then brutally kills each sweet, cute, giggling little girl. I haven't had so much fun since *Back to the Future*.

Not Rated

I FINALLY CALLED my mother that week. I had been leaving it to Max to explain to her where I was when she called, or even to Jean. I decided it was time to explain to her myself and give her my new phone number.

I prepared what I was going to say to her, leaving out Jean entirely. If Max and I ever got back together, I didn't want my parents holding that against him. Still, I was expecting an outburst from her end.

Instead I got, "Well, you know, Ellie, I'm sure you expect me to be upset, but all I'm feeling is relief."

"Relief?"

"We never did feel Max was right for you."

"Mother, we've been married seven years. How is it you've never mentioned this before?"

"We didn't want you to feel we were criticizing your husband."

"What didn't you like about him?" I asked, all ready to defend Max. Or maybe I was just going to defend my choice of Max.

"It wasn't a question of liking or disliking him. It was just that he was always so intense."

I noted that she was already referring to him in the past tense.

"I like intense men."

"I'm sure you do, dear, but they don't wear well."

"I'm the one who apparently didn't wear well," I told her. "He's involved with someone else."

"Ellie, honey, I'm sorry to hear that. You want to fly out here for a visit? Your father and I will be glad to pay for your ticket."

I thought of clean ocean beaches, cool nights and low humidity. I thought of having to listen to my family talk about the big mistake I had made. I decided to stay in New York. I told her to keep the offer open, though, as I might change my mind any day.

I realized after I hung up that I hadn't been thinking of revenge much lately. Oh, once in a while it would cross my mind, but I was no longer obsessed with the notion. Nor was I giving much thought to Max of late. It didn't seem possible that after being with him constantly for seven years I could get over him so easily, and yet I seemed to be doing just that. I found that it was almost a relief not to be living with someone who was so perfect and always finding fault with me. No one yelled at me anymore for the way I squeezed the toothpaste, or the way I threw my clothes on the chair when I got undressed, or my habit of smoking in bed when I read, or my taste in music. It really was a relief not to have to live up to Max's stringent standards twenty-four hours a day. Maybe I was reverting to the slob I used to be, but why couldn't I be a slob if I wanted to?

It was a real shock to me when I first married Max and found out he ironed his shorts and T-shirts and folded them in thirds in his underwear drawer. He also showered before and after sex, and insisted I do the same. His eggs could never be runny, his butter could never be hard and he insisted that the toilet paper be inserted upside down. It was lucky for him he had the intelligence out of bed and the stamina in bed to keep me interested at all.

When Max surprised me by calling me at work one Thursday, I found I didn't even want to talk to him. In fact I was disappointed because I had expected it to be Sam on the phone. He made small talk for a few moments while I made none, and then he said, "I'm thinking of filing for a divorce."

That shook me up, I admit. I was beginning to enjoy being on my own, but divorce sounded so final. It also sounded like failure, and I hated to admit I had failed at something I had tried so hard to be successful at.

When I didn't say anything, he said, "I'm sorry to break it to you like this. Look, I think we should talk in person."

"I don't want to talk."

"Just meet me after work; we'll have a drink."

Instead, I hung up on him. When he called right back, though, I agreed to meet him for a drink. And then I ran into Woody's office and said, "My husband's divorcing me."

Woody got up from his desk and just stood there, not knowing what to do. "Are you okay?"

"I don't know."

"You're not crying."

"I don't feel like crying. But it's sad, isn't it, Woody? Seven years of my life and I don't even have a child to show for it."

"I didn't know you wanted a child, Ellie."

"That's not the point. I don't even have an apartment, or a dog. I have an ironing board and an iron and an old bathrobe of Max's, and that's it."

"Look on the good side, Ellie. That'll make the divorce a lot easier. At least you won't have a custody battle or have to split up community property."

"I'm a failure, Max. I'm a thirty-five-year-old failure."

"You've got a good job."

"Reviewing horror films? Are you serious? I'm no Janet Maslin."

"Look, you want me to buy you lunch? We'll go for Chinese."

"It's ten o'clock in the morning, Woody. Anyway, I've got a screening."

"Hey, I loved your last review. The one before that, though...."

"I know. I went to the wrong screening by mistake, so I reviewed it, anyway. A robot movie was a nice change of pace."

"Look, you can have all the robot movies from now on."

He made it sound as though he was doing me a favor. Which made me wonder if maybe Max was doing me a favor. I'd probably never get around to making the split final; but in every way but the actual divorce, it now seemed final to me. I certainly wouldn't consider going back to the way things had been, when now, with Sam, I was seeing how they could be. It just seemed so sad that I had lived thirty-five years without ever knowing the difference.

I THINK MAX expected tears. Especially when he told me that he'd already seen a lawyer and the lawyer in question was John Castle, who was a friend of mine, not his.

"Well, Ellie?" he said at one point.

"Well what?"

"I know this is traumatic for you. It is for me, too."

Oddly enough, though, I wasn't feeling the least bit traumatized. I was feeling anger that Max was dealing with this in his usual cool, impersonal way. I was feeling regret that I had failed at something as important as marriage. I was also feeling a little guilt that I couldn't summon up any real feelings for Max anymore.

I looked over at him and wondered how two men who outwardly looked like the same type could be so different underneath.

I wanted to rush home and tell Sam the news, but instead I stayed while Max went into all the details, and then I got on the Seventh Avenue subway and rode it home.

I was thinking the hell with Max. There were better men than him in the world, and Sam seemed to be one of them. I'd ask Sam to go with me to the shore for the weekend and maybe, with a divorce imminent, I could tempt him out of the bottom bunk. It wasn't for revenge anymore; it was because I wanted Sam.

When I knocked on his door and he opened it, though, I could see he was packing to leave. I felt my stomach plummet downward at the thought he was leaving for the Amazon so soon. I hadn't thought he was leaving until August. For some reason I had thought I had all the time in the world with Sam.

He read my expression correctly and said, "Hey, I'm just flying to Colorado for a few days. My dad's having open-heart surgery."

I felt so selfish, but I didn't want him to leave. "Oh, Sam, I'm sorry about that."

"His chances are good. I just want to be there for my mom."

"When will you be back?"

"Probably Tuesday or Wednesday."

It wasn't the time to bring up my impending divorce, not with his father going into the hospital, but I did anyway. "Max is filing for divorce," I said.

He came right over to me and put his arms around me. I felt comfortable there. "Oh, Ellie, poor thing. What a lousy time you're going through."

I tried to summon up a few tears so that I could stay in his arms longer, but they wouldn't seem to come. "Seven years," I mumbled.

"I know just what you're going through. It makes you feel like a failure, doesn't it?"

I nodded my head while at the same time burrowing it further into his chest. He had a hairy chest which made it feel padded and nice.

"I don't suppose quoting divorce statistics would help. That's what my friends did."

I shook my head. "When are you leaving?"

"In about a half hour."

"Tonight?"

"Yes."

I pulled away from him and sat down in his hammock.

"I'd stay if I could, Ellie."

"I'll be okay."

"You sure?"

"I'll miss you, that's all."

"I'll miss you, too. Oh, hell, why don't you just come along with me? I'm sure you can get on the flight."

I brightened up a little at that. Just the fact that he wanted me along made me feel better. There was no way, though, that I could just leave like that. "Thanks, but I can't," I told him.

He wrote down something and handed it to me. "Here's my number in Colorado. Call me if you feel like talking. In fact call me if you don't feel like talking, because I probably will."

"Okay."

"You promise, now."

"Yes."

"And listen, you can use my bathroom while I'm gone."

I stayed there while he finished packing, and then I went out with him while he found a taxi.

As we were standing by the curb, waiting for one to come by, he set down his bag and put his arms around me. "Listen, want some good advice?"

"Sure."

"As soon as I leave, go back upstairs and make out a list of all of Max's bad qualities. And then make a list of all your good qualities and compare them. I'll bet you'll come to some conclusions about which of you should be the one filing for divorce."

"Is that what you did?"

"I tried everything."

"And then I can make a list of your good qualities."

"Now you've got the picture," he said, and then he was kissing me and for a good two minutes neither of us was even looking for a taxi. It was such a warm, loving, altogether satisfying kiss that while it lasted nothing existed in the world but just me and Sam.

After he left, I went up to my room and felt very sorry for myself. Partly because of the divorce, but even more because Sam had just left and I already missed him. I wanted to call someone and talk about how sorry I felt for myself, but I couldn't think of anyone who would want to listen.

I decided that sitting around my room moping wasn't going to make me feel any better, so I changed into shorts and decided to go out to eat. I found a table at a sidewalk café and tried to look like the quintessential single who loves eating alone, but I don't think I fooled anyone. Eating alone just isn't very much fun.

Afterward I stopped at the video store. I usually just looked at the recent movies, but for some reason I stopped at the display of music videos and saw two of U2. I rented them both and could hardly wait to get home and watch them. I still loved them just for themselves, but there was also the added attraction that Sam and I had seen them together.

It did occur to me that it didn't take very much to cheer me up. Obviously I wasn't feeling as much like a failure as I liked to pretend.

On Friday night I drove to New Jersey with Alicia and Richard. Richard had been calling the parks department in New Jersey daily to see the status of the beaches. He was told that they hoped to have them open for the weekend. I was sure they hoped that. If they didn't get them open soon, the businesses that depended on the influx of summer people were going to be in serious trouble.

"Where's Sam this weekend?" Richard asked me, leaning over the passenger seat to talk to me. I saw Alicia wink at me in the rearview mirror.

"He's in Colorado. His dad's getting open-heart surgery."

I thought Richard turned a little white at the news.

"Don't mention hearts," said Alicia. "Richard is always thinking he's getting heart attacks."

"And you're always thinking you're having a nervous breakdown."

"That's because you're always giving me one," said Alicia.

"What's happening with Max?" asked Richard. "You heard from him?"

"He's filing for divorce."

There was dead silence in the car for a few moments, and then Alicia said, "Good. You're better off without him."

"Sam's a much better guy," said Richard.

"It's not a question of Sam or Max," said Alicia, "it's a question of what makes Ellie happy."

"What would make me happy," I said trying to change the subject, "is if the weather would cool off."

"That'd make us all happy," agreed Richard.

"You're not getting seriously involved with Sam, are you?" asked Alicia.

"I like him," I said.

"Well sure," said Alicia, "we all like Sam. I just don't want to see you hurt again."

"He's leaving for the Amazon in August."

"Exactly," said Alicia. "Sam's never around long enough to get serious about anyone."

"Doesn't he ever get involved with women?" I asked.

"His wife hurt him pretty bad," said Richard.

"But that's been over for years."

"He's had a couple of other relationships since then," said Alicia.

I asked her what happened to them.

"It's kind of hard to have a relationship," said Alicia, "when one person is always going off for months at a time."

"Oh, I don't know," said Richard. "If you went off for a few months I wouldn't have to be spending my summer at the beach. A polluted beach at that."

I started thinking about how there was something less than perfect to being part of a couple. One always ended up doing something she or he didn't like just because the other one wanted to. I had spent every summer in the city because Max hated the country. Max had eaten out all the time, which he hated, because I didn't like to cook. You always got invited places together even though only one wanted to go. Once you were a couple you were expected to behave like a couple and personal autonomy was sacrificed along the way.

There should be a better way, but I didn't know what it was.

THE BEACHES were once again closed. We checked them out for ourselves and they were disgusting. Things you wouldn't want seen in your own bathroom wastebasket were strewn along the water line and worse was said to be lurking in the water. The pollution was bad enough that dead fish were washing up on shore at alarming rates.

Richard was incensed. He got the owners of the house on the phone and demanded our money back. They said a deal was a deal and they weren't going to return it. Richard countered by asking for half our money back, telling the owners they could make more rerenting it to some unsuspecting fools who maybe hadn't heard that the beaches were all closed. I was surprised when they agreed to that, especially since Richard was being really obnoxious to them.

When Josh and Claire arrived, we discussed whether to settle for half our money. I was torn between wanting at least two thousand back and hating the thought that that meant each weekend I had spent there had cost me a thousand. I could've spent the weekend in Paris for less money. We all finally agreed to take the money, though, although we were sure that as soon as we did the beaches would clear up.

THAT NIGHT Alicia and I stayed home while the others went to the movies. Alicia had asked if I'd mind hearing her do her monologue again, and I said I'd be glad not to see another movie.

The first time she had done it I had been so impressed that she could get up by herself and do something like that that I hadn't been critical of the content. I also hadn't wanted her to lose confidence in what she was doing. Now, though, I decided to point out the places where my interest flagged and other places where she was so funny I wanted her to slow down a little to give me time to laugh. Her constantly moving around and waving her arms also bothered me.

"What do you think?" she asked me when she had finished.

"Would you mind some suggestions?"

"Of course I don't mind."

"Well, this is only my opinion, you understand."

"Ellie, I'm asking for your opinion because I respect your judgment. You were the best director in film school when we were there."

"Max was the best director," I reminded her.

"I never thought so. He just fooled people into thinking he was because he talked the most."

"First of all," I said, "I'd like it better if you'd sit down while you do it."

"No one will see me if I'm sitting down."

"How about on a stool?" I got up and grabbed one of the bar stools and sat it in the middle of the living room, then tipped one of the lamps so that it was shining on the stool. "Sit here," I said. "Sit still while you do it. You don't need any gestures; your face does it all."

With Alicia on the stool, we went over it again, slowly this time with me stopping her at certain points to tell her to slow down. In the few places where it seemed to drag, I had her cut out some of the narrative. Then I had her go through the whole thing again, the way I told her, and I thought it was vastly improved.

"Is it better?" she asked me.

"I think so, but maybe you should get some other opinions."

"I don't need other opinions. I trust your judgment. I'm doing it next Friday night at the coffee house. Would you rehearse with me this week?"

"I'd love to," I said. I was already picturing her dressed all in black, the spotlight on her face, and this funny story coming out of her expressive face. She needed to get her timing down right, to leave room for laughs so that the next lines were not lost. I was sure she would get lots of laughs; she was funny without even trying.

"Could I see what you've written?" I asked her.

"It's really just an outline. I should be able to do it without it by Friday."

"You're telling stories from your life and mentioning real people. What if you were holding a scrapbook? You could be looking at the scrapbook, reminiscing...I don't know, that's probably a lousy idea."

"I think it's a great idea," said Alicia. "It'll give me something to do with my hands. Otherwise, they're flying all over the place."

"I think you've really got something here," I told her. "I think you're going to have a whole new career."

"I think you like directing."

Alicia was right; I did. When I got home Sunday night I took her outline with me and I turned it into a script. Nothing elaborate, just places for pauses and things like that. I got together with her after work on Monday, Tuesday and Wednesday nights and we went over it and over it, finally taking her notes away from her and letting her get used to holding a scrapbook.

Richard watched it on Wednesday night and was impressed by how it had improved. When Alicia told him what a help I'd been, he said, "You ought to put her name on the flyer as director."

"I didn't do that much," I said.

"Of course she's going to go down as director," said Alicia. "She turned a living room story into a real production."

When I got home that night, Sam's door was open and his light was on. I could feel the anticipation building up in me as I stopped and looked in. I was very glad to see him back.

Sam was in his hammock, giving me a rather detached look.

"When did you get back?" I asked, trying to be cool but hearing the excitement in my voice.

"A little while ago,"

"How's your father?"

"Fine, thanks." But something didn't sound fine.

"Really?"

"He's doing great. It's good of you to ask."

Good of me? What was with all this formality? "He's going to be okay?"

"Yes, he is."

"Are you okay?" I asked him. He wasn't acting like himself.

"Yes. How about you?"

"Oh, I'm fine," I said.

"You were rather upset when I left."

"Was I?" That seemed like a long time ago.

"I gather you didn't need anyone to talk to."

"I didn't want to bother you," I told him.

"I wouldn't have given you the phone number if I hadn't wanted to be bothered."

"I know, Sam, but you were feeling sorry for me, and as it turned out, I was fine."

"Didn't it occur to you I might be worried?"

"I figured you had enough to worry about with your father."

"I'm capable of worrying about both of you at the same time."

"I''m sorry; I should've called."

"It wasn't an obligation," he said.

"I should've called to find out how your father was."

"That isn't why I asked you to call."

"I was at the beach house this weekend."

"I understand," said Sam. "It's difficult to make phone calls from New Jersey. Rather like being in the middle of nowhere. Like the Amazon. Although now that I think of it, I was able to make calls from the Amazon."

"It was rotten of me and I apologize. I'm going to go to my room right now and call you to try to make up for it."

"I don't have a phone," said Sam. "But I accept your apology." He sat up in the hammock.

"We got half our money back on the beach house. The beaches have been closed every weekend."

"Every time I tried to call you, you weren't home."

"I haven't been home much."

"So I gathered."

"You're mad at me, aren't you?"

"I just needed someone to talk to. I guess you were out drowning your sorrows."

"No. Actually, my sorrows didn't last long."

"I guess that's good news."

"I think I'm all over Max."

"Maybe," said Sam, "but probably not. I'd think that occasionally, too, but then something would happen and it would start all over again."

"Alicia thinks I'm better off without him. She thought I should have left him years ago. She thinks I should start meeting men."

"Start?"

"Yes. Well, I mean I've met you, and I met Scott, but she means ... Well, I'm not sure what she means."

"She means someone suitable."

"Yes. She doesn't feel you're in the country enough to be...suitable."

"Well, by all means listen to Alicia. Alicia certainly seems to know what she's talking about."

"Not entirely," I said.

"No?"

"I mean, sometimes people can appear to be unsuitable, when in actuality they suit you perfectly."

Sam began to smile. "Yes, that's often the case, isn't it?"

Then I thought that maybe I'd said too much, come on too strong, so I changed the subject. "I've been rehearsing Alicia." I told him about how I'd been directing her.

"That sounds good. I'm glad you've been keeping busy."

"I think you're mad at me."

"I'm not mad at you," said Sam. "What are you doing this weekend?"

"Why?"

"Some friends invited me to the country. I thought you might like to come along. They have several acres and a stream and it's like being in another world."

"I'd love to," I said, "but Alicia's doing her act at a club Friday night and I want to be there."

"I'd like to see it, too," he said. "We could take the train up Saturday."

"Sam, if you're inviting me along because I took you to see U2, it's not necessary. There's no reason why you should miss Friday night in the country."

"This has nothing to do with U2. Anyway, I'd enjoy the train ride. I like trains."

"Your friends don't mind an extra person?"

"No. They said if I was seeing someone, to bring her along."

"We're not exactly seeing each other."

"No, but I'm not seeing anyone else, either. And you did invite me to the beach for the weekend."

I said, "This is all very complicated and I don't think I like it. Are we dating? What is it we're doing?"

"I think we're getting to know each other."

"It was easier in college."

"Everything's easier in college," Sam agreed.

"In college we would've made love by now."

"Things move faster when you're young."

"Are we going to share a bed?"

"No, we're not, Ellie."

"But you're leaving in August."

"What does that mean, that we quickly have to have an affair before I'm gone?"

When I didn't say anything, he got up out of the hammock and came over to me. He put his hands on my shoulders and squeezed them. "Ellie, what am I going to do with you?"

"Obviously nothing."

"Look, I like to think I'm also looking out for your welfare, but I admit I'm primarily protecting myself."

"From me?"

"From anything that's going to make it difficult for me to leave."

"How can you be so... *controlled*?"

"At the moment, it's not easy."

I put my arms around him and lifted my face.

"You testing my control?" he asked.

"Yes."

He sighed, and then his mouth closed over mine, and in the end it was me who had to break away, as someone had to show a little control.

But it wasn't easy.

Chapter Eleven

Review/FILM
THE GUMMY BEARS
by Ellie Thomas

At last a summer film that the whole family can enjoy. Milos Backman has directed a cunning comedy
about a package of gummy bears that has been left
in a laboratory overnight and, during the night,
some toxic fumes invade the bag and bring the
gummy bears to life. After that it's all laughs as the
gummy bears, trying to make friends with the
townspeople, manage to stick themselves to the
people and nothing will pry them apart. A sterling
performance by Shirley Insane as the sheriff's wife,
who falls in love with the gummy bear stuck to her,
will no doubt garner her another Academy Award
nomination.

Rated R

THE COFFEE POT CAFÉ was located in the basement of
a church in Greenwich Village. Alicia was doing her act
at ten and Sam and I got there around nine-thirty, not
expecting many people. Instead, the place was packed; a

large number of people was standing at the back behind the tables. A folk singer straight out of the sixties was playing the guitar and singing a song about an idiot savant. We bought coffee and went back outside to have a cigarette and wait for Alicia to come on.

Some of the crowd cleared out after the folk singer was finished, and we were able to get a table. Richard joined us with a big bowl of popcorn, and then the lights dimmed and a spotlight came on, hitting a single stool sitting in the middle of the performance area.

Alicia came out carrying her scrapbook. She was dressed in black jeans and a black T-shirt and her dark brown hair was hanging loose to her shoulders. The spotlight washed out any color she might have in her face and she looked fragile and rather poetic.

She sat down on the stool, crossed one leg and balanced the scrapbook on her lap. She smiled at the audience, opened the book and then began her story. She was utterly charming and had the audience with her from her first words. They laughed a lot and smiled a lot and nodded in agreement over some of the observations she made. She never stumbled over a word or faltered over a phrase and it was as though she had been doing this every night for years. I was very proud of her. I had seen Spaulding Grey do similar performance art and I found Alicia much more appealing.

It lasted an hour and I think the audience would have sat still for twice that amount. Afterward we walked over to the Lion's Head for drinks and Richard and Sam were amazed at how much she had improved her performance.

"Thanks to my director," said Alicia, giving me a hug, and I realized that I had made a difference in the performance and that I hadn't forgotten what I'd once known about directing. Still, even without me, I think the performance would have been wonderful.

"That was good work," Sam said to me as we walked home, hand in hand.

"Thanks."

"Makes you feel good, doesn't it?"

"I know what you're trying to do, Sam."

"I'm just complimenting you, that's all."

"You're trying to get me to admit that doing good work is more satisfying than anything else."

"Is that what I'm trying to do?"

"You're trying to justify living half your life in the jungle."

"I don't have to justify that."

"There's more to life than work," I said.

"I know. But if you really love your work, that's got to come first."

I wondered if it was like that with all men, that they all left you feeling like you came in a poor second. But then coming first might be a real responsibility. I wasn't sure I'd want that kind of responsibility over someone else's life. And maybe men didn't, either.

SAM AND I caught the train at Grand Central the next morning. It was a two-hour ride up to Columbia County in upstate New York. Once we left the city behind we seemed to be in another world. It was as startling a change as when Dorothy went from black-and-white Kansas to Technicolor Oz. I had forgotten that dwellings could be set so far apart from each other and that there were still places where trees weren't routinely cut down and fields left undeveloped. I wasn't one of those who yearn for a quieter life in the country, but it wasn't a bad thing to be able to get away for an occasional weekend.

Carol and Michael and their two small boys met us at the train station. Carol, a skinny blonde in her late thirties with her hair in a long braid, threw herself into Sam's arms and gave him a big hug. Michael was a bear of a man with a huge chest and a sweet face and the two boys, about three and four, had their mother's skinny build and their father's face. Michael introduced himself and then the boys, but I never did get their names straight.

We drove to their house in an old station wagon with Carol squeezed between the two men in the front seat and me in the back with the boys. I could see that Carol was leaning into Sam and they seemed to know each other far better than Sam knew Michael. There was a familiarity between them that seemed to go beyond friendship, but I thought I might be reading something into her friendliness that wasn't there. I don't come into contact with children much and had always supposed I liked them, but the two in the back seat with me did nothing but whine and complain and crawl back and forth across me during the drive.

Carol and Michael had bought an old farmhouse and several acres and Michael was trying his hand at farming while Carol rewrote other people's screenplays. Sam had told me Michael used to be a studio musician but they both had gotten tired of the city and wanted to bring up the kids in the country.

We spent the day alternating between watching Michael do his chores and watching Carol try to keep her children entertained while she flirted with Sam at the same time. I felt myself getting jealous at one point and left them alone to go in search of Michael. He was hacking away at some weeds with a big sharp tool and it wasn't very interesting to watch, but I nonetheless stood there for at least twenty minutes and pretended an interest. By that time I decided there was no reason why I should be jealous of Sam and Carol since I wasn't involved with Sam myself and since Carol had a perfectly nice husband. And then I countered that argument with the fact that while I might not think I was involved with him, I was certainly spending a lot of time with him, and while she had a perfectly nice husband, she obviously preferred Sam's company at the moment. And whether I should be jealous was academic anyway. The fact was I was jealous.

At times in the past I had pictured Max and me living in the country with children, and at the time it had seemed idyllic. Now that I was in the midst of it, I could see it wouldn't suit me at all. Of course my children would be perfectly behaved and my place in the country wouldn't require so much work.

They did manage to get the kids to bed that evening before we ate, and then Michael barbecued chicken and we had a wonderful meal on their screened-in porch. The conversation involved people they all knew, so I tuned out and just enjoyed the sound of crickets, which was something I had never heard before.

Shortly after the sun went down, Michael and Carol got up and I thought perhaps we'd be going in the house to play cards or maybe watch television. Instead, they excused themselves and went to bed, telling us to stay up as late as we liked.

Sam and I spent about a half hour cleaning up and doing the dishes. Then he looked at me and said, "You ready for bed?"

"Not really, are you?"

"I don't know what else there is to do. I guess we could go for a walk."

"There aren't any sidewalks and there aren't any lights," I pointed out.

Sam folded the dish towel and hung it over the counter to dry. "We'll do whatever you want to do."

"What do you do at night on the Amazon?"

"Sleep. But then I'm usually up at dawn."

"I'd never be able to sleep this early."

"Let's take a walk. We can follow the road out in front; maybe it will lead to a town."

"And if it doesn't?"

"Where's your sense of adventure, Ellie? Come on, we'll explore Columbia County."

I changed into jeans and a long-sleeved T-shirt so that I wouldn't get eaten alive by mosquitoes, and then we set off. The moon was out and we could see perfectly well on the road, but except for the occasional house, we walked for over an hour and didn't come to anything that remotely resembled a town.

It was enjoyable, though. We held hands and Sam told me what it had been like growing up in Colorado and about skiing, and I told him of a childhood spent on the beach and my surfing exploits. He was relaxing and easier to be with than Max, who always wanted some kind of action to be going on. It was like being alone in that there was time for my own thoughts, but better than being alone because I could share them.

I was feeling very close to him but I wasn't prepared for it when he put his arms around me and kissed me. Especially since this kiss had all the sexual passion in it that our others had lacked. For one thing, our mouths both opened and our tongues began to explore, and there's a whole different feeling to that than just kissing with your mouths closed. Except for Max I hadn't kissed a man like that in years and at first it felt as if I was doing something wrong. I suddenly realized that I was standing by a deserted road in the middle of nowhere and beginning to feel the kind of passion that I usually felt only when making love. What's more, it was obvious that Sam was feeling the same way.

We both backed off from the kiss at the same time and stood staring at each other. And then, without either of us saying anything, we went back in each other's arms and kissed again, and this time I was filled with a wild longing.

When I finally broke away a second time, it was only to lay my head against his chest. My heart was pounding and so was his and the night suddenly felt full of possibilities.

Sam spoke first. "I want you to know I don't just kiss anyone like that."

I felt myself relaxing and lifted my head. He was smiling.

He went on. "Just because the moon is out and the air is fragrant and you happen to be the only woman within kissing distance didn't have anything to do with it."

"Of course not," I agreed.

"Anyone else would have gotten my standard brand, friendly kiss."

"The one I usually get."

"Exactly."

"You lost control."

"Yes, I did."

"Are you sorry?"

"I'll show you how sorry I am," he said, starting to kiss me again.

It felt like the Fourth of July, only the fireworks were going off in my body. Maybe, just maybe, Max had made me feel like this once, but I wouldn't bet on it. The chemistry with Sam was even more surprising since I also felt he was my friend. Friends, in my experience, didn't feel like this about each other.

Sam finally broke off to say, "I don't know what's happening here, Ellie, but it's going to take some thinking about. And the fact that we've been given separate bedrooms will give us plenty of time to think."

Carol had made a point of giving us separate bedrooms at some distance from each other. At the time I had thought that Sam requested it. Now I wasn't so sure.

And then, because the moment was so perfect I couldn't handle it, I had to go digging around and spoil things. "Did you ever go out with Carol?" I asked him.

I expected an immediate denial, but instead he was silent.

"You did, didn't you?" I said.

"It was a long time ago," he said.

"How long?"

"Before she married Michael."

"How long was that?"

"About six years."

I stepped away from him, more jealous than I had any right to be. "You brought me up here to spend the weekend with an old girlfriend of yours?"

"An old friend."

"That's not the way I see it."

"I don't have that many old girlfriends, but I've stayed friends with them all."

I tried to imagine Max and me remaining friends, but I couldn't. "Who broke it off?"

"She did."

I wasn't sure I believed him. "What happened?"

"Nothing happened. We wanted different things, that's all."

"I see."

"She wanted a house in the country and children and I wanted to make my films about the rain forest."

Well, I didn't want a house in the country and children, but I also didn't want to get seriously involved with someone who liked to spend most of his time in the rain forest.

"You should've told me," I said.

"I'm telling you now."

"You should've told me before we came up. I might not care to spend the weekend with one of your old lovers."

"I don't honestly think of her that way. I think of Carol and Michael as friends, and I thought you'd enjoy it up here."

"It's boring," I said, suddenly angry with him. I wasn't angry over the fact that he had once gone with Carol. I was angry because I suddenly realized how much I had come to care for him and now he was telling me that he wasn't interested in getting involved with anyone, that he was a free spirit who preferred the jungle to the company of a woman. I was being rejected again, but this time before I was even accepted.

"Let's go back," I said, turning around and heading back up the road. I was walking fast but he caught up to me with his long, slow stride and when he took my hand I let him. I wasn't mad at him. I was mad at myself for momentarily spoiling things between us.

Even holding hands was different. There was something between us now that hadn't been there before and it was a strong sexual attraction. I could feel it in the dampness of his hand where before it had been dry. I could feel it in the way that just the touch of his hand was now sending signals to the rest of my body. Where before I had found him appealing, where before I enjoyed being friends with him, where before I had appreciated his warmth and concern and his good nature, now I was finding him amazingly sexy and it was all I could do not to turn to him on the road and cling to him once more.

I could not recall being this sexually excited since the day on the lake in Central Park with Max. There is something about the build-up of sexual tension before you make love for the first time that is never repeated. Other things take its place, but that initial excitement is never again duplicated. It was the very best of feelings; it was also the most frustrating by far.

He didn't speak and I was afraid to. I was feeling rejected, I was jealous over Carol out of all proportion, and I knew that anything I said would reflect these things and make me sound catty.

The noise of the crickets began to get on my nerves. I thought I had read somewhere that crickets made that noise when they were mating. I was probably wrong. If it was true, though, then it ticked me off that billions of crickets were at that very moment doing what I wanted to do and none of the male crickets were saying to the female crickets, "Not tonight, dear, we have separate bedrooms."

I couldn't help it, I started to laugh.

"What's funny?" asked Sam.

"The crickets."

"I see."

"They sound like they're having a good time."

I heard Sam's low chuckle. "They're interesting insects."

"Oh, fascinating," I agreed. "I'm surprised you haven't done a documentary on them."

I could feel the rumble of his laughter as it extended to his hand. "Maybe I like animals because they're so uncomplicated."

"Maybe you like running away from reality and hiding in the jungle."

"Oh, no—it's very real down there."

"No women, just insects."

I felt his hand tighten up. "Who said there weren't any women down there?"

I pictured native women with bare breasts. Bare, sagging breasts according to *National Geographic*. "You have an Indian girlfriend?"

"Who said all the women down there were Indians?"

"How many white women are living in the jungle?"

"You'd be surprised," said Sam.

"For all I know you have a wife and a dozen kids down there."

"No wife. No kids."

"But a girlfriend."

"Relax. Most of the white women in the jungle are missionaries."

"I've seen movies about missionaries. They're not all nuns."

"I feel rather the same about missionaries as I do about animals in zoos. Both are out of place and both should be returned to their natural habitat."

"What's the matter, Sam, the missionary women give you a hard time?"

"No. They just confuse the Indians."

I was sure that was a subject he could go on about for hours, but I decided he could save it for a future documentary. I was more interested in his love life. "You said *most* of the white women were missionaries. What about the others?"

"We get occasional bird watchers and even an explorer or two."

"No one on a permanent basis?"

"In the towns, but not in the jungle."

"Towns? You mean it's civilized down there?"

"To me the jungle's more civilized than the towns, but yes, there are towns. Even cities."

Somehow I liked the idea of him alone in the jungle better than the idea of his proximity to cities. "Damn it, Sam, do you have a girlfriend down there or not?"

"No. No girlfriend."

I breathed a silent sigh of relief. If there's anything I hate, it's competition.

"Do I sense some jealousy on your part?" asked Sam.

I thought of denying it, but ended up saying, "Yes."

"Good. You've got to care in order to be jealous."

I let him sweat it out a minute before saying, "I care."

"So do I."

"I'm beginning to care so much it's scaring me."

"I know. It's the letting go of control. It's rather like flying."

"And you can always crash," I said, thinking of coming home and finding Max and Jean that day.

"But the alternative's even worse," said Sam. "Never taking a chance is like never even living."

I WAS TAKING the sheets off the guest bed the next morning when Carol came into the room.

"You don't need to do that," she said.

The odd thing was, if I hadn't found out she and Sam had had an affair, I probably wouldn't have bothered. But now that she was competition of a sort, I was out to make a sterling impression. I woke up imbued with the desire to be the perfect house guest, even if we were leaving that day.

When she saw that I wasn't going to desist, she started to help me, pulling off pillowcases as I pulled off sheets, and then going to fetch clean sheets for the next guest.

As we remade the bed together I could sense from her attitude that she was also feeling competitive and was not going to allow me to one-up her. She even offered to help me pack and seemed thwarted when I pointed to my already packed bag.

"It's been fun having you up here," she said. "It's nice talking to city people for a change."

"It's been lovely getting out of the city," I told her.

"You must have Sam bring you up again."

"I had a share in a beach house but the beaches have been closed to swimming all summer."

"You should've tried our stream," she said. "The water's so clear we could drink it."

This seemed strange as there was bottled water in their refrigerator. "I like to surf," I said.

"Oh, well then...."

"Are the men back from the store yet?"

"No, they aren't." She appeared to be listening for a moment for the sound of a car. The men had taken the boys with them and it appeared that she was stuck with me.

"Can I help you fix breakfast?"

She gave me a tentative smile. "Not until they get here with the eggs. But thanks. I have coffee ready, though, if you'd like a cup."

"I'd love one," I said.

I followed her out of the room, gathering up the pillowcase full of dirty bedding on the way out.

She turned at the head of the stairs and saw it. "Just leave it there," she said. "I do the wash on Mondays."

I suddenly didn't like what I was doing, which was trying to score points off the other woman. She was married, wasn't the other woman at all, and I was behaving badly.

As we went into the kitchen, I said, "Carol, Sam told me about the two of you last night. I hadn't known."

I thought her face lightened somewhat. As she poured me a cup of coffee she said, "Oh, I thought you knew."

"No. He didn't say anything."

"That's just like Sam. Any other man would have been bragging about it all the way up, trying to get you jealous."

"I suppose you're right."

"He's still very dear to me. I don't mean that I have a secret passion for him; my husband is the only man I'm passionate about. But I think that Sam and I will always be close friends."

It seemed to me that she had an old-fashioned way of speaking and I wondered whether it was something she had picked up in the country or whether she had always talked like that. "I feel that way, too," I said. "That Sam and I will always be friends. I haven't known him very long but I already feel as though we're friends."

Her look was curious. "You're not lovers, then?"

"No."

"Oh. I thought perhaps you were."

Then why put us in separate bedrooms? I wanted to ask. "I've just recently separated from my husband," I said, as though in explanation.

"Oh, I'm sorry."

"He left me for a friend of mine." I was asking for sympathy, a trait I detest in others, but I couldn't seem to help it. Next I'd probably start crying.

"If Michael did that to me, I'd kill him."

I'm sure my eyes lit up at that. "Would you?"

"Absolutely. And her, too."

"I was quite obsessed with revenge," I told her. "But I seem to be getting over it."

"I imagine Sam is very comforting."

"Yes, he is. That's exactly the right word for it."

"He's the nicest man I've ever known. Nice in the sense that he genuinely cares about people."

"Yes, you don't meet many men like that."

"Not in New York, anyway."

"Would you mind my asking you a personal question?" I said. "You needn't feel obliged to answer."

"I did," she said.

"What?"

"I was the one who broke up with Sam. Sam doesn't like endings."

"But didn't you love him?"

"Very much. I broke up thinking that he'd be so brokenhearted that he'd give up his traveling and beg me to settle down. I think he knew that, too, but decided to let me keep my pride and not make him reject me."

"If you loved him, why didn't you travel with him?"

"And live in the middle of a jungle somewhere? What kind of life would that be? Anyway, I wanted children, and I couldn't picture myself squatting down in some patch of dirt and giving birth. I like living in the country, but I also like having a hospital nearby."

She started in then on her ordeal giving birth to her first son and was well into her twelfth hour of labor when I heard a car pull up outside. I was very relieved. While I had enjoyed my conversation with Carol, nothing drives me up the wall faster than hearing women telling childbirth stories. You'd think that each one of them personally invented the process.

When Sam entered the kitchen, my smile toward him was of such warm relief, that I'm sure he was left wondering.

"THAT WAS FUN," I said to Sam on the train. "Thank you for bringing me." I moved a little in my seat so that our shoulders were touching. It gave me an instant gut reaction.

"I thought you were bored," he said.

"It's nice being bored occasionally. The trouble with the city is that you're never allowed any time to be thoroughly bored. It's restful." I moved my left hand onto my thigh so that it was very close to Sam's hand and he could hold it if he felt like it. He did more than that, picking it up and pressing it down on his thigh, causing a shiver to go through me.

"Good. We can do it again if you want." He moved his leg so that the length of it was up against mine. I felt a shiver run up my leg and pass through my body. It felt so good, I wanted it to happen again.

I said, "The air was so clean. Have you noticed how bad the air's gotten in New York this summer?" I shifted a little so that my breast brushed against his chest. I stayed like that a moment, then moved away and waited to see if he would follow. He did, his body turning so that we once again touched. Just the mere touch of my breasts against his chest caused signals to be relayed to all parts of my body.

"I thought it was always like that," said Sam, his thigh tensing and untensing against my hand, making me itchy to move my hand around the terrain. I wondered if he'd jump out of the seat if I moved it due north.

"No, it's gotten much worse. When it gets that bad in California they tell you to stay indoors, but they never say anything about it in New York." My fingers began to move against his thigh. The car was empty except for us and I could see that Sam had noted this fact when his arm went around me and pulled me close.

"You should see the smog in Denver," said Sam. "Every time I go back it's gotten worse."

The temperature in the train was rising at an alarming rate. I slowly moved my hand up his chest and rested in the V-neck of his T-shirt. My fingers slid inside and I brushed my knuckles against the hair. I wanted to rip off his T-shirt and bury my face in his chest.

He did nothing for a moment, then slid down in the seat a little and pulled me over so that my head rested against his neck. "You don't have to tell me about smog," I said. "I grew up in California." It was an effort by now to keep up my part of the conversation.

Sam's lips went to the top of my head and pressed against my hair. His hand was now moving mine along the inside of his thigh. It was sending chills through me, so I could imagine what it was doing to him.

"There's no smog in the Amazon," he murmured.

I curved my hand so that my fingernails were scratching his thigh. My own thighs were almost imperceptively clenching and unclenching and my clothes felt heavy and warm. I leaned in toward him so that my hair brushed against his ear. "Oh? Why is that?"

His hand snaked up beneath my T-shirt and sandpapery fingers began to slowly circle one nipple. My chest felt constricted as he replied, "No smog-causing agents."

I shifted a little more, turning my upper body and pressing against his fingers. I could feel the heat coming off his body, or maybe it was off mine. "How hot do you suppose it is in the city today?" I wondered why we needed this inane conversation.

Sam let go of my hand and I thought, *Oh, hell,* but then I felt his hand moving up the inside of my thigh, causing temors along all my fault lines. I began to move my hand to the top of his thigh, slowly, teasing him, wondering how I had gotten to be such a tease.

"I don't know how hot it is in the city today, Ellie, but we're certainly managing to heat things up in this air-conditioned car."

"What do you mean?" All innocence.

"Are you trying to drive me crazy?"

"Maybe. You're sure driving me crazy."

"Ellie, we're on public transportation." But his hands were still moving and doing wonderful things to my senses.

I moved my hand into his crotch and heard him groan, and then he was moving in his seat until our bodies were pressed together. Our mouths were already open when they met, one of my hands opening his zipper, one of his reaching up under my shorts. You would have thought we'd both just come out of a year-long stay in the jungle, our desperation was that great. I moved my legs and his hand slid up inside my panties; he shifted a little and I had his zipper down and my hand was reaching for his erection just as his fingers were sliding inside of me. I was instantly off and flying, my insides folding and unfolding, layer after layer, bringing me deeper and deeper inside of myself until, at last, reason returned.

He was holding me tightly, rocking me in his arms, when I heard him say, "Oh, oh, we're pulling into a station."

Sanity returned with a whistle and the sound of brakes.

Chapter Twelve

Review/FILM
CLOSE ENCOUNTERS IN CENTRAL PARK
by Ellie Thomas

In the role of her career, Kathleen Turnip plays a shy, unattractive secretary who works in a large, impersonal corporation. While strolling through Central Park on her lunch hour one day, a flying saucer lands at her feet. She is soon beamed up into the spaceship and her life is changed forever. In this stunningly realistic film brought to us by the able director, Milos Backman, Ms. Turnip gives the performance of her career as the shy secretary who is transformed into a femme fatale and becomes the president of the corporation.

Rated X

"I HAVE TO FLY to the coast after the Fourth," said Sam. "My film's entered in a festival in San Francisco."

We were at one of my favorite restaurants in the Village. There was a chance of running into Max and Jean, as Max had always liked the food, too, but that wasn't why I had taken Sam there. I had wanted him to like the same places I liked, and so far he seemed to be enjoying it.

"How long will you be gone?" I asked.

"About a week, I guess."

He'd be leaving for the Amazon the beginning of August and not seeing him for one of the remaining weeks was something I didn't want to contemplate. I thought of my mother's offer of a plane ticket out.

"I was thinking of going home for the Fourth of July," I said, trying to sound casual and not at all as though I was about to manipulate him. "Why don't you come to Southern California for a few days with me before flying to San Francisco?"

If he felt manipulated, at least he was looking pleased about it. "I could spend a long weekend there, I guess. Can your folks put me up?"

"There's plenty of room," I said.

Sam smiled his slow, lazy smile. "I'd like to see where you come from."

"I'd like to show you around."

"Will they be upset, your showing up with a man before you're even divorced?"

"I don't think so. I gather they weren't all that crazy about Max."

"You *gather*? Don't you know?"

"I thought they liked him, but now it appears they didn't. They only met him twice—once at our wedding in California and once when they visited about three years ago. They came to visit us in New York and Max insisted they stay at a hotel. They never really got to know him."

After dinner we walked through Washington Square Park. There were roller skaters and musicians and old men playing chess, and I thought Sam would like it, but after the third dealer tried to sell him drugs, he steered me out of the park, shaking his head. "This city's getting worse every day," he said.

It was, of course. The heat still hadn't let up, the homeless were sleeping in every available place, and murders were up by several percentage points. Still, as far as I was concerned, it made every other place seem boring.

As we walked up Sixth Avenue, I stopped at one of the banks to take some money out of the machine. When the electronically controlled door opened, I saw at least a half dozen people sleeping inside. It made me a little nervous, and if Sam hadn't been with me, I don't know whether I would have risked taking out money. There was also the guilt at having money to take out when the homeless were all around me on the floor. When I heard a baby cry, the guilt became extreme, and I handed the mother a twenty dollar bill. Max would've had a heart attack if I had done that when he was with me, but Sam reached into his pocket and gave her a few more dollars.

"Something should be done about them," said Sam when we were back out on the street.

"Why don't you make a documentary about them?"

He shook his head. "My thing's the rain forest. If something isn't done to save that, we won't have an earth and the homeless problem will be gone."

And then he was talking about the rain forest again and I felt as if I had lost him. He was almost obsessive on the subject and it made me wish that I felt that passionately about something. It seemed to me as though women were only that passionate and obsessive about men while men put all that energy into their work.

I'VE NEVER SEEN such a scaredy-cat. Sam was tense, his hands grasping the armrests until his knuckles turned white, before the plane even began to taxi toward the runway. I reserve such fear for the dentist.

"Relax," I told him, transferring my cigarettes, lighter and magazines into the pocket on the back of the seat in front of me and then storing my handbag under the seat.

"I'm relaxed," he said, his voice soft from having little air behind it.

I had the window seat and Sam asked me to pull down the shade.

"Sam, I like to watch when we take off."

I fastened my seat belt and then took a good look at him. He looked panicked. I could not imagine that he flew as often as he did if he always panicked. Once would be enough for me.

I reached for his hand and held it. It was cold and sweaty at the same time. "I suppose you know I'm madly in love with you," I said.

There was no reaction whatsoever.

"Unbeknownst to you, my divorce is already final and even now my mother is planning our wedding in California."

"Umm," said Sam, or at least it sounded like *umm*

"Nothing fancy, nothing spectacular. My mother says that isn't suitable for a second wedding. Just a tasteful little ceremony at home with a few friends in. And family, of course."

Sam made a noise as though he was clearing his throat. Then, as the plane's engines started up, he turned white and closed his eyes.

"I thought we'd honeymoon in Ensenada. It's very romantic down there and the language will make you feel at home. You do speak Spanish, don't you?"

I could feel Sam's hand tremble. Nothing I was saying was even getting through to him. I felt so sorry for him;

he seemed paralyzed with fear. I pushed the armrest that separated us back against the seats, then put my arms around him and pulled him as close as the seat belts would allow.

"Is anything the matter?" asked one of the flight attendants.

"Could I get a drink for him?" I asked.

"It's not allowed before take-off."

"He's having a very bad anxiety attack," I told her. "Anything would do."

She looked down at Sam in sympathy, then walked toward the back of the plane. A few moments later she returned with one of those small bottles. She surreptitiously handed it to me and I smiled my thanks.

"Here, Sam," I said, holding the bottle to his mouth.

He wasn't so paralyzed that he wasn't able to take two swallows of the scotch, not even flinching as he drank it. His color slowly returned and before the plane took off he had visibly relaxed.

"I'm sorry," he said, "I'm not usually that bad."

"How can you fly around when you feel like that?"

"I'm okay once I get a drink. I tried a tranquilizer once and that worked, but I didn't want to get in the habit." He then noticed that the armrest was gone and my arms were still around him. That brought a smile to his face.

I stopped holding on to him and divided us with the arm rest once again. I didn't think we should risk a recurrence of the train incident. Not in a crowded plane. "You're really okay now?"

"I still think we're going to crash, but once I've had a drink I don't care anymore."

"Sam, it's statistically safer than driving the freeways in California."

"I know that. I know all the statistics. But I still can't help thinking that whatever is holding it up in the air is going to suddenly give way and we're going to fall."

"I don't think I want to get into this subject," I said, as the plane took off, shuddering all the way.

"I don't mind prop planes," said Sam. "It's these big ones where you can't even see the pilot that bother me. For all I know they're up there playing chess and not even watching where they're going."

"I don't think the average pilot is smart enough to play chess," I said.

"Great," said Sam. He started to look nervous again, so I handed over the bottle.

WE LANDED in smoggy L.A. to perfect weather. My brother, Pete, picked us up at the airport, took one look at Sam and looked confused. As he leaned down to pick up my bag, he whispered to me, "I thought you and Max broke up."

"This is Sam, Pete," I said to him. "Sam, this is Pete, who just confused you with Max."

"I'm older," said Sam, shaking Pete's hand.

"I haven't seen Max in a few years," said Pete, still looking as though he thought I was playing a joke on him.

"You will probably never see him again," I said, following him out of the airport.

I opened the passenger window as Pete drove south on the freeway. The exhaust fumes weren't great, but the mild air was. We were out of Woody Allen territory and it felt strange to be back.

I looked forward to a whole week of never sweating. A whole week of Dad watching the sports channel on cable TV. A whole week of Mom trying to get me to cut my hair because she had some notion that from age thirty on, women were supposed to have short hair, preferably permed. A whole week of old high school friends finding out I'm in town and calling me to come over and see their 3.2 children. A whole week of such perfect weather you prayed for an earthquake just to stir things up.

Sam, in the back seat, looked stunned by the bumper-to-bumper traffic. "Is it always like this?" he asked.

"It's almost rush hour," said Pete, leaving Sam, no doubt, to wonder what happened when rush hour actually arrived. I could've told him—nothing happens. The cars just sit there.

I was itching to drive. The urge never hit me in New York. Most of us New Yorkers who were brought up elsewhere like to say that one of the best things about the city is you don't need a car. It's true you don't need one, and if you have one you can't afford to park it, but the urge to drive never leaves you. What is particularly annoying is that the people you pay to drive you around the city—cab drivers, bus drivers, subway conductors—don't know how to drive. You know if you had the chance, you could do it a hundred times better. I was eager to get home, ask Dad for the keys to the car and take off down Pacific Coast Highway with the wind blowing through the car and the radio tuned to 1010 ROCK on the dial.

Pete and Sam were carrying on a conversation. Pete had asked Sam what he did and when he heard documentary films, he changed the subject. I doubt Pete had ever seen a documentary film. Sam asked Pete what he did, and when Pete said engineering, Sam changed the subject. Now they were both discussing skiing, which left me out because the only time I went I chickened out on the lift and had to be pushed off and refused to go up in it again. My idea of a good time skiing is sitting in the lodge toasting marshmallows.

When we turned off onto Seal Beach Boulevard and headed for the ocean, nostalgia washed over me like a wave. As far as I'm concerned, the only thing that Manhattan lacks in order to make it perfect is a beach with six-foot waves. If we had that, though, we'd probably be mugged when we tried to surf.

I hung out the window as we drove down Main Street in case I saw anyone I knew. I didn't, though, and I was still hanging out when we pulled up into my parents' driveway. Mom must have been watching out the front window because she came out of the door as soon as we pulled up.

She had dropped fifteen pounds since I last saw her and her hair was a little blonder. She had a great tan and looked better in shorts than I did, and the first thing she said to Sam was, "You must be Jim."

"Sam," I said to her.

"I always get those names mixed up," said Mom, giving Sam a kiss on the cheek and then saying to me, "He looks a lot like Max."

"Maybe I ought to shave off my beard before I meet anyone else," said Sam.

"I'll show you where the bathroom is," said Mom.

"He's only kidding; he's not going to shave his beard," I told her.

Mom made a point of showing Sam to the guest room, which used to be my bedroom. I looked in at it and saw that Mom had set out framed pictures of me at every age for Sam's viewing pleasure. Sam picked up one, looked at it, then looked at me. I was ten in the picture. My pigtails stuck out beneath a baseball cap worn backward. I had scabs on my knees and was crossing my eyes for the camera. I could remember the day my mother took the picture. I had just come home from the playground where the older boys had let me play outfield after pestering them for an hour. I had this big crush on a sixth grader, Matt King, who hit the ball harder and farther than any of the other boys and who always wore his baseball cap turned backward. He spit in the dirt and cursed a lot and I wanted to be just like him. In fact I wanted to be him. I had come home, cursed at my mother, spit in the kitchen sink, and instead of yelling at me, she had laughed and taken that picture.

"You look like you were a brat," he said.

"That's how I wanted to look."

He went over for a closer look at my high school graduation picture. It wasn't representative of the way I looked in high school because it was the only time I hadn't been wearing jeans and a big shirt. Instead, I was dressed in one of Mom's suits, trying my best to look at least old enough to get served. I remember practicing what I thought was a sexy look in the mirror until I could do it without watching myself. So instead of smiling, as the photographer had requested, I was looking at the camera with my sultry look, only I turned out looking half asleep instead of sexy. My hair, which was parted in the middle and down to my waist at that time, was lighter than it had ever been since leaving California and the sun.

"I wonder if we would've dated if I'd known you in high school," said Sam.

"Not likely," I said. "My folks wouldn't have let me date someone as old as you."

"Keep rubbing it in."

"Anyway, I only dated surfers."

"We didn't do much surfing in the mountains."

"Where were you when I was eighteen?"

He thought for several moments. "New Guinea."

"Making documentaries?"

"At that age, I still thought I could be a filmmaker-explorer. Over in Europe they can make a living doing that, making their film and then showing it and lecturing to sell-out crowds."

"Was that before you wanted to save the rain forest?"

"At that age, all I wanted was adventure."

I was sleeping down the hall in what was called my mother's sewing room, although I'd never known her to sew in my life. I think it's where she went to talk to her friends on the phone while my dad watched sports.

"Your father's out on the patio getting the barbecue ready," Mom told me when Sam and I walked back to the kitchen. "Go out and say hello."

I introduced Dad to Sam and at least he didn't mention any resemblance to Max. Probably because he'd never paid much attention to Max. As soon as he found out Max didn't like sports, that was it. I had a pretty good idea Sam didn't like sports, either. If you see a guy in the summer as often as I'd seen him, and if he never mentions what place the Mets or the Yankees are in, it's a pretty good indication.

We went down the steps to the beach and sat down in the sand. There were still some surfers out, young kids, not much more than twelve or thirteen, but they were riding the waves like pros. I had no idea whether I could still do it or whether, like riding a bike, it was something you never forgot.

"It's nice here," said Sam.

"It was the perfect place to grow up."

"That's the way I feel about Colorado."

"Would you want to go back?"

"You mean to live?"

I nodded.

"Hell no. Would you?"

"No. But it's nice to know it's here all the same."

"Do your parents keep trying to get you to move back?" he asked.

"They never give up. You'll probably hear all the arguments at dinner tonight: Clean air, less crime, bigger apartments, not as much stress. And, of course, they're right on all counts."

"I keep hearing about moving back, settling down and having children."

"Oh, I get that, too," I said. "Particularly the part about children."

"It's beautiful here," said Sam. "Why *do* you prefer New York?"

"After a few years there, every other place seems boring. Anyway, it might look like paradise here with the ocean and the palm trees, but the air isn't any better, there's just as much crime, the apartments might be easier to find but they cost just as much, and there's more stress involved in driving the freeways than there is taking a subway. I guess New York is to me what the jungle is to you."

"I'd like to save the jungle."

"Yes, well, I'd like to save New York, too, but I guess I'll leave that to Donald Trump."

MY TWO OLDER BROTHERS came over to dinner with their wives and kids. They carried the picnic tables out of the garage and set them up on the patio. I could remember how embarrassed I was the first time Max had dinner with my family. The conversation was all about sports and TV shows and how bad the traffic was getting on the freeways and I could sense how bored Max was, how bourgeois he thought my family. Max and his friends never engaged in small talk while they ate. It was always film criticism or philosophy or radical political movements. It was always intellectual and very, very worthwhile. They had made me feel stupid at the time, and I was always afraid to set forth any opinion in case it would be wrong and they'd laugh at me. Gradually I not only learned what the correct opinions were, I grew bored with the conversation.

Now I didn't even think about it. They talked about the price of car insurance and how the Dodgers were doing and the city council voting to keep a proposed McDonald's off the highway, and I didn't think Sam was bored, but even if he was, I didn't care. If he wanted more stimulating conversation, all he had to do was initiate it. A couple of times one or another of my nephews would call Sam "Uncle Max" and someone would correct him, and then a little while later it would happen again. Afterward, one by one, my brothers and their wives came up to me and told me, in confidence, that they really liked Sam. No one had ever said that about Max.

We had a great time for the next three days. We went to Disneyland one day and to the Laguna Beach Art Festival one night, and the rest of the time we just hung out at the house, going swimming and sitting around on the beach and even going to the supermarket with my mom. At the end of that time, my family loved him, even if I hadn't quite made up my mind. I was absolutely crazy about him and could get aroused just looking at him, but I wasn't ready yet to cross over the line of love. I was sure that if I started thinking of it as love I'd be devastated when he left the country.

The night before he was to leave, though, I knew I didn't want him to. What I wanted was for him to invite me up to San Francisco, but he hadn't even hinted at it.

I got his clothes out of the dryer for him and then I sat on the bed and watched him pack his few things into his canvas bag. Sam packed a lot lighter than I did. I never knew what to take so I always ended up taking everything.

"I'm sorry you're leaving already," I said to him.

"Well, with me out of the way, you'll be able to visit with your family."

"You want me to iron anything for you?"

"What's the point of ironing anything if I'm just going to pack it?"

"What hotel are you staying at?"

"I'm staying with my sister."

"You have a sister in San Francisco?"

"Cleo. She's a few years younger than me."

"Is she married?"

"Nope. Never been married. Cleo's the free spirit in the family."

"What does she do?"

"She's the girls' volleyball coach at San Francisco State."

I instantly pictured a jock with a whistle around her neck. "That sounds like fun," I said.

"It's not just playing games," he said. "She travels all over recruiting high school players."

"I didn't know it was that serious," I said. "I thought it was just a game you played at the beach."

"She says it's big-time these days."

"I envy you," I said, none too subtly. "I love San Francisco in the summer."

"Why don't you come up?" asked Sam, as though it was the most natural thing in the world.

"You mean with you?"

"Sure. Cleo's got plenty of room."

"I'd just be in your way," I said, already planning how to break the news to my parents.

"I love having you in my way. I would've mentioned it but I figured the last thing you wanted to do on your vacation was go to another film festival."

"You really want me to come?"

"Don't you know how I feel about you by now?"

"Not really," I said.

I thought he was going to tell me he loved me, but he didn't. He just gave me a hug and said, "I'd love to have you come along. And that way you can hold my hand on the plane."

"Never mind holding your hand," I said, "I'm going to sneak you a bottle on board."

CLEO WAS A MINIATURE version of Sam without the beard. She didn't have a whistle around her neck, but she had great muscle tone and an even greater apartment. It was the top floor of a Victorian house in the Marina District with lots of windows and a spectacular view out of each one. Where there weren't windows, there were hanging plants and all of them looked healthy. Every plant I ever bought in New York died within a week.

I envied Cleo her life-style. During the time we were there, she had four dates with four different guys, each of them better than anything you ever see on the streets of New York. Her apartment was perfection and was continuously filled with a large circle of friends who were always dropping by. She was a great cook, played the drums in a women's rock band on the weekends, and in her spare time took photographs of San Francisco that she sold to postcard companies. She seemed to have everything going for her and enjoyed it all.

I HAD THROWN a dress in my suitcase when I packed for California. I hadn't anticipated needing one, but in case the situation arose, I didn't want to have to buy a new one. I was glad I had packed it when I got to San Francisco, as people in that city dressed up for things like film festivals, unlike their counterparts in New York.

Unfortunately clothes hold memories. It wasn't until I pulled the dress out of my suitcase and laid it across the bed in Cleo's guest room that this fact hit me.

It was a simple dress made of silk, which made it ideal for traveling. It was black, short, very proper in the front with a high neck, but the back was open and plunged to the waistline. It hit me just above my knee. Because of the low back, the dress necessitated my going without a bra, which was no big deal as the front was full and by no means transparent. If I moved a certain way in it, though—maybe bent a bit when sitting down and certainly if I moved on the dance floor—the dress would fall forward and the curved sides of my breasts would show. Believe me, there were far more daring dresses in the store, but there was something about this dress, maybe the fact that it did look prim and proper until I moved in a certain way, that seemed to drive Max crazy.

Draped across the bed it was just a dress, but as soon as I put it on it became a documentary of my past. The first time I had worn it, Max and I were on our way out of the apartment, going to some faculty party, as I recall, and as I turned back to make sure the door was locked, the dress did its falling forward act. Max, who was often impulsive sexually at the most inopportune times, slid his hand into the side of the dress, and the next thing I knew we were back in the apartment and making love on the living room floor. We never did get to the party. After that, there was something almost magical about its effect on Max.

As soon as these memories came back, my first thought was to take it off and wear something else. Not that I had anything else that was suitable, but I was sure that Cleo would lend me something. And then I thought, *No*. Taking it off would mean that Max still had some sort of hold over me, and I refused to admit that possibility. The hell with Max, I would keep it on. After all, it was only a dress.

Sam's eyes widened when I appeared in the dress. "You look lovely," he said, and at first I thought the dress was working its magic on him, but then I realized it was the first time he'd ever seen me in anything but shorts or jeans. My hair had gotten sun streaks from just the few hours at the beach and I wore it hanging loose. I knew that with my hair light and a good tan black was very becoming.

Cleo came out wearing a low-cut, frothy white creation and looking as unlike a jock as possible. Sam put an arm around each of us and said, "I've got to be the luckiest guy in San Francisco tonight." I dipped forward a little, seeing if Sam would suddenly decide to give up the film festival and rush me into the nearest bedroom, but Sam missed the dip and all I received was a raised eyebrow and a smile from Cleo.

I had always loved Sam's documentaries but I had no idea how well-known and respected he was until we arrived at the film festival the first night and he was besieged by fans. More impressive were the other professionals who came up to him and told him how much they liked his work.

I sat through his army ant movie for the third time, only this time I stayed awake. It was simply brilliant. I vowed to print a retraction of my former review and write an apology that would appear in *Views*. Comparing the army ants to Sherman's army got laughs out of everybody, and by the time the film was over I had learned as much about the Civil War and the South as I had about army ants and the jungle.

It was no surprise to me when Sam's film won the top award. There were other excellent films, but none was nearly as good. What did surprise me was the jealousy I felt. As he accepted the award, as the audience went wild, as the photographers vied for the best position in which to take his picture, as the reporters moved in to interview him, I felt like a real failure.

I stood there in my black dress, looking as pretty as I was ever going to look, maybe even looking sexy. I stood there with no other achievement than that Sam had brought me. I stood there knowing that all I had accomplished in thirty-five years was one marriage that had failed and a lot of idiotic reviews, when what I most wanted at that moment was to be up there accepting an award for best documentary. I wanted to be someone, not just a reviewer of second-rate movies for a second-rate newspaper.

And in the moment that Sam accepted the award, looking handsome and sexy and even kind of distinguished, when the audience went from hushed silence to wild applause, when I heard him speaking with the kind of knowledge and self-assurance I could never hope for, I fell hopelessly in love with him.

Chapter Thirteen

Film/REVIEW
THE WITCHES OF EAST 76TH STREET
by Ellie Thomas

Take three Upper East Side Yuppies (Chair, Susan Saranwrap and Michelle Fizzle), make them so bored with their co-ops, their summer homes in the Hamptons and their stock portfolios that they have nothing better to do than summon up the devil (Danny DePita), have each of them seduce him, each seduction sillier than the last, and you have this summer's major bomb in *The Witches of East 76th Street*. The talents of all (to say nothing of the $35 million budget) could have been better put to use doing something about the homeless. At least the homeless won't have to endure the two and a half hours running time of this tedious film.

Rated PG

NEW YORK didn't get any better that summer. When I got back from California, everyone asked, "Why did you come back? I would've stayed out there."

The heat got worse. The electric company was forced into having daily brown-outs because no one was turning his air-conditioning off. There were a few black-outs, one in my neighborhood. The beaches also got worse and people suddenly started to get interested in the environment. Even the movies seemed to get worse.

And my relationship with Sam wasn't progressing, either. Sam was as warm and as friendly and as interested in me as he had been when we first met. We kissed a lot, sure, and at times we took it a few steps further. But what we were actually doing was frustrating the hell out of each other. I knew he was afraid of really letting himself go, as he did on the train, and I knew the reason was that he was leaving soon. I didn't push it, either, because I knew that if we ever spent the night together, I'd do everything in my power to prevent him from leaving.

I didn't tell him I was in love with him. Once in a while I was tempted, just to see if I could get a rise out of him more than anything else. I resisted the impulse, though, because I wasn't eager to be rejected. Anyway, I doubted that he'd believe me. Since it took him so long to get over his ex, I was sure he thought it would take me just as long. I had this feeling he thought that any day now I would go back to Max.

I was, though. Over Max, that is. Once in a while something would remind me of him, but most of the time it was as though he had never existed. There was nothing like a new love to make the old fade away. And what I had with Sam was so much more satisfying that what I'd had with Max; there was no comparison.

I had found something that took the place of my fantasies of revenge. It was my plan for Sam. Like my revenge strategies, it kept me awake at night, but not all night.

I had hit upon the plan in bed one night as I was trying to figure out how to get Sam to fall in love with me. I half suspected that he already was and was refusing to admit to it, but I wasn't positive. And after my experience of assuming my marriage was okay, I wasn't going to be caught believing in assumptions again.

I wanted to prove to him that I was perfect for him. I wanted to make myself so indispensable to him, so crucial to his happiness and well-being, that he wouldn't leave me behind when it came time for him to leave.

I started off with the kind of housewifely things that I was used to doing for Max. Whenever I went to do laundry, I stopped by his room and asked if I could take anything of his.

The first time I asked, he said, "Thanks, Ellie, but I can do it."

"I'm going anyway," I insisted, "and I don't have enough for a full load." I did have enough, but I had left half of it back in my room so I'd have room for his.

"Why don't I go along with you?"

"Why should two of us have to suffer?" I countered.

"All right," he said, "if you really don't mind." He gathered up some towels and underwear and shoved them into my laundry bag.

I couldn't believe the way I acted at the laundromat that day. I was so thrilled that my underwear was mixing it up with his underwear, that I watched them tumbling about in the dryer with as much concentration as I ever watched a movie. Surely they looked good together, I told myself, seeing bras getting tangled in shorts and T-shirts meshing with T-shirts.

The next time he insisted on doing both our laundry and I couldn't talk him out of it. This wasn't the plan. He wasn't the one who was supposed to become indispensable.

I bought a cookbook that supposedly taught one to become a sixty-minute gourmet cook. I started stopping at the supermarket after the screenings, carrying home enough food to feed me and Sam with a lot left over.

The first time, I knocked on Sam's door, and when he opened it I said, "I'm cooking dinner for us tonight."

"Sounds great," said Sam, immediately joining me in the kitchen. It turned out he could cook gourmet meals in just sixty-minutes without the benefit of a cookbook, and while we ate in a lot after that, Sam ended up doing most of the cooking. I did the dishes. No one's better at doing dishes than I am.

I discerned that Sam and Max were miles apart when it came to domesticity. Max had gone from having his mother take care of him to having me take care of him, and he rarely lent a helping hand. Sam was more self-sufficient than I was and didn't really like anyone fussing over him.

Next I started checking out books about the Amazon at the library. During this phase I didn't lose any sleep because those boring tomes put me right to sleep at night. I tried to engage Sam in conversation about the Amazon, but since I was going by the books and he was going by experience, my conversational skills were more geared to classroom questions than to dinner table talk.

While Sam and I had previously argued over nearly everything, now I agreed with everything he said, laughed at all his silly remarks, and asked him countless questions about his work. This came to an end when I discerned that I was beginning to bore him.

My final attempt was when I tried to interest him in letting me write a book about the making of one of his documentaries.

"Have you ever written a book?" he asked me.

"Well, no..."

"I doubt whether you'd get an advance from a publisher on that idea, then," he said.

Everyone was saying how slow the summer was going, how they thought it would never end. I couldn't believe how quickly the time was passing. Before I knew it, it was the end of July and I knew that Sam would be leaving any day.

I called Alicia in a panic and asked if she'd meet me for a drink.

"He's leaving, Alicia," I said before she even sat down.

"You mean Sam?"

"Yes." I could tell I was sounding shrill and tried to calm down.

"When?" she asked.

"I don't know. Any day now."

"He'll be back, Ellie."

"But I don't want him to leave."

"Hey, calm down, have a drink."

We called the bartender over and ordered wine coolers, and I managed to get a cigarette lit after three aborted tries. I knew the end was approaching and I didn't know what to do to stop it.

"What am I going to do?" I asked Alicia.

"I didn't know you felt this way about him. I thought you were still getting over Max."

"I'm in love with him," I confessed.

"Are you sure?" Alicia, ever the skeptic.

"Of course I'm sure. I never even think about Max anymore."

"I don't know, Ellie, I would think you could use a little breathing space."

"I don't want any breathing space. I want to go down to the Amazon with Sam and live with him."

"What would you do down there?"

"I could help him. I could take care of him."

"You'd probably be the one needing to be taken care of down there. What do you know about jungles?"

I didn't feel inclined to rattle off all the facts I had learned. "I don't know what I'll do if he leaves me."

"Ellie, have you thought this out? Is this really what you want to do with your life?"

"All I want is to be with Sam."

Alicia gave me a dubious look. "I don't think so, Ellie."

"I know how I feel."

"I don't think you want to be with him. I think you want to *be* him, just the way you wanted to be Max when you married him."

"That's nonsense," I said, having expected sympathy from my friend, not criticism.

"You're the one who wanted to make documentaries, Ellie, but as soon as you met Max and let him talk you into thinking he could do it better than you, you just caved in and wrapped yourself up in his life."

"That's not what I'm doing with Sam."

"That's exactly what you're doing. You should've seen yourself when you were telling me about him getting that award in California. You weren't feeling pride and love. You were feeling envy. You think you can't do it and so you want a man who can."

"You really don't understand, Alicia."

"I think you're the one who doesn't understand."

Well, things got worse after that and we ended up splitting from the bar and making our separate ways home. Just because Alicia was suddenly doing something with her life, she thought everyone should be like her. Sure I wanted to make documentaries, but let's face it: if I were a documentary filmmaker I would have made one by now.

And Sam was so very, very talented.

SAM MADE A POINT of asking me out to dinner the next night. This probably doesn't sound out of the ordinary, but it was. We had eaten dinner together every night since we had been back from San Francisco with the exception of the night before, when I had been in such a foul mood after my drink with Alicia that I hadn't had dinner at all.

"Sure," I said.

"I meant somewhere special," said Sam, and my heart began to sink. I knew he didn't mean special in that he was going to propose to me. Anyway, I was still married. I was sure he meant special in that it might be the last chance we'd get to do it.

"Are we dressing up?" I asked him.

"Why not?" said Sam.

I showered and changed into a leopard-patterned silk jumpsuit—would it remind him of the jungle?—and pinned my hair on top of my head.

Sam looked right out of *Casablanca* in a cream-colored linen suit and a tan silk shirt. I couldn't imagine that this gorgeous outfit had been packed away in that bag of his. He looked stunning.

He winked at me. "The old man looks pretty good when he dresses up, doesn't he?" he asked.

"I don't think I would've recognized you."

"You don't look bad yourself," he said, sizing me up in the silk jumpsuit. He reached up and pulled the pins out of my hair so that my hair came tumbling down around my shoulders. "That's better," he said. "That gives you that wild, abandoned look."

I felt like pointing out that I would have been glad to be wild and abandoned with him anytime during the past several weeks. His move gave me hope, though. I began to think that it wasn't a farewell dinner at all. I began to hope that instead it was a prelude to a seduction.

Sam had made reservations at Tavern on the Green and we walked there through the park, holding hands. It was still miserably hot and humid but I no longer noticed. I was noticing the way he kept glancing down at me, as though in approval; the way his hand tightened on mine every so often; the way our hips brushed up against each other's as we walked.

We were seated in the glass room with the view of the park. Sam ordered champagne.

The view out the windows was beautiful but I'm afraid I couldn't take my eyes off Sam. I was in love and no longer trying to hide it.

When the champagne was poured, Sam lifted his glass and said, "To a memorable summer."

I would have preferred that he say "To us," but I lifted my own glass and then drank from it.

As the food was served and we ate, Sam kept calling forth memories of the times we'd had together: the weekend at the beach house, the walk in the country, the Matterhorn ride at Disneyland. I thought they were a little too recent to be reminiscing over, but I went along with it.

We had just ordered coffee and strawberries and cream when Sam said, "I'm going to miss you, Ellie."

"But you don't have to, Sam," I said, leaning across the table toward him.

Sam looked a little startled. "I know I don't have to, but I will nonetheless. I've really loved this summer."

He loves the worst summer in the history of New York, but he doesn't love me? *Come on, Sam,* I thought, *spit it out.*

"I wish—" he began.

"You wish what?"

"Oh, nothing."

"You wish what, Sam?"

"I don't know. I hate leaving people, and now I'm going to be leaving you."

"Take me with you." The words were out of my mouth before I had time to retract them.

Sam sank back in his chair.

"I mean it, Sam. Let me go with you."

Sam sounded slightly flustered as he said, "There aren't any movies to review in the jungle."

"Good. I'm sick of reviewing movies."

"Ellie, I'll be in the middle of nowhere. There would be nothing for you to do."

"I've thought about it," I told him, "and I could be your assistant."

"I don't need an assistant."

"I could carry your equipment and help you set up your shots—"

"Ellie, that's what *I* do."

"I could cook for you, Sam, and do your wash—"

"I can do that myself or get an Indian woman to do it."

"Wouldn't you rather have me?"

"Ellie, you're too intelligent a woman to come down there and be my slave."

"I don't mind." I was pleading now and I could see the distress in his eyes.

"Ellie, the answer is no."

I sat back in my chair, fighting tears. "Why have you been spending all this time with me if you don't want me around?" I asked.

"I love having you around," he said, "but I'm going down there to work. I work from the time the sun comes up until when it goes down, and then I sleep."

"But I love you, Sam." I was so embarrassed to be saying this to him, but I seemed to have no control left at all.

"You really don't, Ellie."

"Yes, I do!"

"Ellie, you're still getting over—"

"Don't say Max because I'm all over Max."

"This is called love on the rebound, Ellie, and I know because it happened to me."

"I know when I'm in love."

"So do I, and I'm in love with you."

I caught my breath. "Oh, Sam . . ."

"And if it's really love, it'll still be there when I come back. But I'm not holding you to anything, Ellie, because I think it's really too soon for you to know."

"How do I know you'll come back?"

"I always come back."

"If you really loved me, you'd take me with you."

"Ellie, honey, listen to me. You've got to do what you want with your life, not take over mine."

"I'm not trying to take over your life. I just want to be part of it. And I think you're only saying you love me at this late date just to get me off your back."

He was looking distressed when he said, "I think you're going to regret this, Ellie."

"I already regret it," I said, pushing back my chair and running out of the restaurant, passing the waiter carrying our strawberries along the way.

I ran through Central Park as though a mugger was after me, causing some stares as I ran. I was so humiliated. I had begged him to take me, and he had turned me down. No man seemed to want me as a permanent part of his life.

I couldn't go home. He was so nice he'd probably be the one to do the apologizing, and I didn't want to be around for that. Instead I called Alicia when I got to Broadway, and she said I could spend the night on their couch.

I BORROWED some of Alicia's clothes for work the next day so I wouldn't have to go home. By day's end, though, I knew that I owed Sam an apology. He had been a true friend to me all summer when I needed one, and I had repaid him by embarrassing him in public. No wonder men didn't want me.

When I got home that evening, I went straight to his room. The door was open and the room was empty. I was so sure he couldn't have left like that, that I ran to find Philippa and asked her where he was.

"Sam left today," she told me.

"What time?"

"This afternoon. I'm surprised you didn't know."

"Did he leave a message for me?"

She shook her head and I could see the pity in her eyes. God, maybe I did need a healer.

When I got to my room there was an envelope shoved under the door. It reminded me so forcibly of the note

Max had shoved under our door that it took me a few minutes before I had the nerve to pick it up. When I did, it said:

Dear Ellie,
I'm sorry I upset you last night. I had wanted it to be a perfect evening. Get on with your life and I'll be back before you know it.

Sam

At the bottom he put where he could be reached in care of the Amazon Camp in Iquitos, Peru.

I crumpled up the note and threw it across the room.

ALICIA STOPPED BY to see me unexpectedly a few days after Sam left. She was the first person to knock on my door since Sam's nightly knocks, and for a moment I held my breath the feeling of déjà vu was so strong.

Then I yelled, "It's open," and Alicia walked in.

"This isn't bad," she said, looking around.

"It's all right."

"I thought I would hear from you. What are you doing, becoming reclusive?"

"I wish I could just say the hell with men, Alicia, but I really love him."

"I warned you that Sam's not around for long. But he always comes back."

"But I want him all the time."

"Then you'll have to settle for someone boring like Richard. Or Max. The interesting ones won't be tied down."

"I don't want another Max," I said.

"Then be glad for what you have."

"I don't have *anything*."

"You've got a very good, very close relationship with one of the best men I know. Come on, Ellie, you're finally free after seven years of subjugation to Max. Why can't you enjoy yourself?"

"It's your fault for ever inviting me to that party."

"I didn't have Sam in mind when I invited you. I just wanted to get you out of the house. And speaking of houses, come on, I have something to show you."

"What?"

"We'll take a little ride and I'll show you."

"Alicia, I'm in no mood for shopping."

"Good, 'cause the stores aren't open tonight."

"I'm not going anywhere unless you tell me first where we're going."

"And you think you're adventurous enough to live in the jungle?"

I got up from the couch and grabbed my handbag. "Okay, let's go."

Alicia broke down and told me during the walk down to Seventy-sixth Street. "I've got a sublet for you, if you're interested."

"Are you serious?"

"Unless you want to stay in Philippa's place. Your room's better than I thought it would be."

"Tell me about it."

"It's a two-year furnished sublet—one bedroom, small terrace, two cats—"

"A *terrace*?"

"Small."

"Can I sit out on it?"

"Oh, yes. You can even eat on it. It gets filthy, though, from the exhaust."

"Who cares?"

"The owner's a friend of mine. He 's got a grant to work and study in Germany for two years."

"Can I afford it?"

"If you'll take care of his cats and forward his mail, he'll let you have it for what he's paying, which is about the same as your room at Philippa's. Plus, there won't be a security deposit."

"I assume it's air-conditioned."

"Of course."

I was suddenly cheered up, and it made me feel like a traitor. I guess it was mostly the thought of an air-conditioned apartment, but partly, I think, because I was getting tired of always being brokenhearted over men. I didn't mind missing Sam, but I hated the thought that I was turning into a martyr.

TWENTY MINUTES into *The Computer That Took Over the World*, I could not stand one more second of it and I got up and walked out. A taxi pulled over to the curb the first time I stuck my arm out, and fifteen minutes later I was walking into Woody's office.

"Hey, Ellie," he said, "back so soon?"

"I'm quitting," I announced.

Sweat broke out on Woody's upper lip. "Sit down, make yourself comfortable, Ellie. I wasn't complaining."

"I am."

"What's the problem?"

"Woody, I am totally burnt out on horror flicks. I would rather sell tokens in a subway station, and I hear it pays better."

"Ellie, baby, you'd get mugged down there."

"Being mugged couldn't be any worse than sitting through trash like *The Computer That Took Over the World*."

"Is that the new Disney—"

"I'm not discussing it."

"But, Ellie, you're our most popular reviewer."

"Oh? Then why do I have the smallest office and have to review the worst movies?"

"You and horror movies go together. You're almost a cult figure in certain circles."

I stood up. "Have my check ready, Woody. I'm clearing out my cubicle."

I was halfway to my office when Woody caught up to me. I continued into my room and began to look around to see what I wanted to take with me. There wasn't anything.

"Ellie, I've been tossing around this idea."

I ignored him.

"What I was thinking is, maybe you'd like to write a weekly column. Pick any subject, as long as it relates to film."

I turned to look at him. "Are you serious?"

"Yeah. I think it's a great idea."

"And I wouldn't have to review any more movies?"

"Well, maybe occasionally. But you could pick the ones you wanted to review."

"Not horror movies."

"No, I'm talking films. Maybe even foreign if you wanted."

"I don't know, Woody."

"And you can have a bigger office."

"I don't need a bigger office; I prefer working at home. I got an apartment, did I tell you?"

"In the city?"

I nodded.

"Wow! Good for you."

"I could use a raise, though."

"Twenty-five a week?"

I didn't answer him because I was in shock. Would it have been this easy all the time and I hadn't known it?

Mistaking my shock for greed, Woody said, "And an extra ten bucks for every movie you review."

"I want to see this in writing," I told him, finding myself wishing that Sam could see me now. I had an idea he would've been proud of me.

I WAS SITTING in my air-conditioned living room curled up on the down-filled couch, one gray cat beside me and a black one perched behind my head, when I got the idea.

Alicia had done her act twice more, once in another coffee house and once in a comedy club. Both audiences had loved it. I picked up the phone and called her.

"Hey," said Alicia, "I loved that article you wrote about the new British movies."

"Thanks," I said. "Listen, I just had an idea."

"You doing okay over there?"

"I love it. You know it's the first time in my life I've ever lived alone? I went from my parents' house to a dorm with you to living with Max."

"There was your room at Philippa's."

"That doesn't count. It was just like being back in the dorm."

"So you're getting into being single, huh?"

"I think I could learn to love this. How about you and Richard coming over to dinner this weekend?"

"We'd love it. So what was your idea?"

"Alicia, listen . . . I don't want you to think I'm trying to steal your thunder."

"What thunder is that?"

"Well, hell, you've got your own thing going and I'm really jealous."

"You have nothing to be jealous about. I think you're doing great with those articles. Vincent Canby better watch out."

"*Views* is not quite in the same league as the *Times*."

"You always were too good for that paper."

"Alicia, I want to make a documentary of your act."

"Are you kidding me?"

"If Spaulding Grey can do it, why not us? I think you're much funnier than he is."

"But it's just me on a stage."

"I've got some ideas about that."

"Now you've got me so excited I'll never get to sleep."

"Do you have to go to sleep?" I asked her.

"No."

"Good. Come on over. I think we ought to talk about this."

I GOT THE FIRST POSTCARD from Sam the next day. It had a picture on the front of a llama, and the scenery looked more mountainous than jungly. He asked me how I was doing, said work was going well but he missed me and signed it "love." A few weeks before, I would have agonized over what he meant by that. Now, for the first time, I believed it could be true. I still loved him, but it no longer bordered on an obsession, and I was beginning to realize that life could go on with Sam on the Amazon and it could even be good. Maybe not quite as good as if he was with me, but good enough so that I no longer felt like putting my life on hold until he returned. And if he asked me now to give up my air-conditioned apartment with my own terrace to camp out in the jungle with him, I doubted I'd jump at the chance.

The next day I bought five picture postcards: one showed Madison Square Garden, and I wrote him a little message on it telling him about all the rock concerts he was missing; one was of the zoo and I told him the polar bears were missing him; a third had a picture of Lincoln Center, and I wished him good luck on his documentary; the fourth had a picture of a pretty apartment building with terraces and I put my new address on it; and the last one—and it hadn't been easy to find—had a picture of a train. I didn't write anything on that one, hoping he'd use his imagination.

GETTING BY on four hours' sleep a night, I had the first draft of a shooting script ready when Alicia and Richard came over to dinner on Saturday night. As they sat over coffee, I read it to them, then waited for their reactions.

"I didn't know you could write film scripts," said Richard.

"You should've seen her student film," said Alicia.

"What do you think?" I asked.

"I love those voice-overs you put in," said Alicia, "about how the act transpired. The part set in the beach house is a riot."

"I don't envision it as just your act," I said, "but more the story of how you get an act together in the first place."

"The thing is," said Alicia, "you should probably get an actress to play me."

"No," I told her, "you're perfect."

"You're always acting," said Richard, which won him a punch in the arm from Alicia.

"I'd like to do it sixteen-millimeter black and white," I said. "I liked the look of U2's *Rattle and Hum*."

"With it suddenly blossoming into color at some point?" asked Alicia.

"No, no color."

"How're you going to finance it?" asked Richard.

"I was thinking maybe... Oh, hell, I was thinking maybe Max could lend me the equipment from NYU."

"You wouldn't mind asking him?" asked Alicia.

"Why should I? He owes me one."

"The expensive part is the film," said Richard.

I nodded. "I thought I'd start looking for grant money."

"I might be able to get the financing," said Richard.

Alicia and I both turned to him.

"For a credit," he said.

"We'll put you down as 'best boy,'" said Alicia.

When they left that night, Alicia gave me a hug. "It's about time you got your life in gear," she whispered in my ear.

"You know something? I think you're right."

I felt like writing Sam a letter that night, telling him all about it. But then I thought it might be more fun to wait and surprise him.

MAX SOUNDED surprisingly glad to hear from me when I called him.

"How's it going?" he asked me.

"It's going great, Max. I have a favor to ask of you."

There was rather a long pause before he said, "What?"

"I'm making a documentary and I'm trying to keep the costs down. I was wondering if you could loan me a sixteen-millimeter from the university."

"*You're* making a documentary?"

"That's right."

"Why don't you borrow Sam Wiley's camera?"

"Because he's in the Amazon using it himself."

There was a pause, then, "Yeah, I think I can arrange it."

"Good. Let me know and I'll come down and pick it up."

"I'll bring it to you."

"You don't need to do that."

"I have to see you anyway. I've got the divorce papers for you to sign."

"Oh, great," I said, and found I meant it. It was time to cut the ties to the past.

MAX SHOWED UP with his beard shaved off. I had never seen him beardless and I couldn't take my eyes off his face.

"Aren't you going to ask me in?" he asked.

"Oh, sure, of course," I said, moving aside so that he could walk in the door. He looked ridiculous. I don't think I ever would've married him if I'd seen him clean-shaven. He had a weak chin and what looked like acne scars along his jaw.

"You shaved your beard," I said, as one of the cats wound around his legs. He looked down nervously for a moment as though he'd never seen a cat before.

"Yeah," he said, "I had to. I got a mild case of eczema, and the doctor told me to shave it off until the weather got cooler. Damn weather's enough to give anyone a rash."

"It's starting to cool off a little," I said. "Actually it's quite nice on the terrace. Do you want to go out there?"

He blanched. "You have a terrace?"

"Just a small one." I led him outside to where my "small" terrace held a chaise longue and a low table and two chairs. "Can I get you a drink?" I asked.

"If you're having one."

"Well, no, I'm not," I told him for maybe the first time in his experience. Usually I would have a drink just to keep him company.

"So you're making a film."

"That's right. A documentary."

"Well, lots of luck."

"I'll invite you to a screening when I get it done. So. You said something about divorce papers for me to sign."

He suddenly sat forward in the chair, hands between his knees, staring at me. I noticed that his eyes looked a little glazed as though he hadn't been getting much sleep.

In contrast to his forward motion, I leaned back in my chair. "How's Jean?" I asked, and was surprised to find myself smothering a yawn as I said her name. His eyes widened at the sight of the yawn, which I'm sure he could tell was genuine.

"What?" he said.

"I asked how Jean is."

"She's in Texas."

"Really? Visiting her family?"

"I just got back from there."

"I thought you looked tan."

He gave his bare arms a self-conscious appraisal.

"Did you have good weather?"

"Hot, but compared to here," he began and then stopped with a look that clearly said, *What the hell is going on here?*

"Less humidity, though, I imagine."

"We split up," he said abruptly.

I couldn't think of anything to say to that, so I waited for a further explanation.

He waited, too. And then, when nothing was forth-coming, he looked at me and said, "I really screwed up, Ellie."

"How was that?" I asked politely, wondering if he perhaps cheated on Jean, too, but not caring one way or another.

"Leaving you for her."

"I wouldn't worry about that," I said, and saw him turn a little pale.

Max started to wring his hands rather dramatically. "Ellie?"

"What?"

"I'd like to get back with you."

"No way," I said, and saw the way the words made him cringe. I softened it with, "Well, after all, Max, I was the innocent party."

"I guess I hurt you pretty bad."

"Yes." I looked out at the buildings across the street. "But I'm over it now."

I heard his breath catch, and then he said, "It's Sam, isn't it?"

"Not at all. I love my apartment, I love the way my career's going, and I guess I'm enjoying life. I wouldn't change it for anything."

"I think you're putting up a brave front."

I laughed so hard at that that I'm sure I was heard clear across the street. When I finally got myself under control, I said, "Let me have the divorce papers, Max."

"I didn't bring them. I thought I could talk you out of it."

"Well, messenger them to me tomorrow, would you? And Max, thanks for getting the camera for me."

FIVE POSTCARDS arrived in the mail from Sam.

The first had a picture of two Indians paddling in a

dugout canoe. Sam wrote on the back that this was the Amazonian subway system, and while not as fast as its New York counterpart, it was far more pleasurable. The second postcard showed a bamboo floating house. He said that while, like the rooms at Philippa's, it wasn't air-conditioned, it was a whole lot cheaper. The third was a picture of an ocelot, and Sam's message on this one was to the effect that they had an open zoo down there. The fourth was a colorful picture of parrots. Sam wrote on the back that this was the local rock group and that concerts were free. The fifth postcard showed a train winding around the side of a mountain. There was no message on that one, just several exclamation points on the back.

I immediately got together a care package for Sam and mailed it down to Peru. I enclosed a U2 T-shirt; a small battery-operated fan; a book, *Burden of Dreams*, about a documentary made about Werner Herzog's film that was shot near where Sam was living; a recent copy of *New York* Magazine; and a small No Smoking sign to make him feel as though he hadn't left civilization. I also enclosed the weekly columns on film that I had written in his absence. I didn't enclose a letter because I was afraid if I sat down and wrote one, it would end up mushy and sentimental and would be the last thing he wanted to read. I did, however, enclose a few chocolate bars, which would probably arrive mushy enough.

I HAD FINISHED filming and editing and had come in under budget when my divorce became final. Autumn was in the air and suddenly New York was the most beautiful of all cities. It wasn't perfect, though, because Sam wasn't there with me.

Being free felt wonderful. I wanted to celebrate it and thought of calling Alicia, but instead, on an impulse, I picked up the phone and called my travel agent. I loved Sam more than ever, and now I knew I could love him on his terms. In fact I don't think I would have settled for any other way.

Next stop: Iquitos, Peru.

Chapter Fourteen

I arrived in Iquitos, Peru, with a footlocker, a large suitcase and a carry-on bag. I planned on staying a week. I had already gone through Customs in Lima where the Customs inspectors insisted on inspecting every item I had brought along and gave me looks as though I was clearly crazy.

The flight from Lima had been astonishing. For what seemed like thousands of miles we flew low over the jungle, an unbroken expanse of green that seemed never-ending. The casual attitude of the flight attendants and the passengers was also a novelty. No seats were assigned and you could smoke wherever you liked. No one bothered with a seat belt, and people were moving around the plane the entire trip. It felt more like a party than a flight. When we landed, there was a rush for the door and I waited in my seat until the stampede was over.

Once through Customs, six small boys hoisted my trunk and carried it out of the terminal. A man who looked like one of the homeless in New York grabbed my suitcase. Several other men tried to take my smaller bag away from me, but since it was fastened to me by a strap that went across my chest, they didn't succeed.

When I got outside the building, the heat and humidity enveloped me. It was very much the way New York had been all summer except that the air quality was a lot better. I saw that my trunk was already being strapped on top of a Volkswagen that I hoped was a taxi. I handed out money all around, received many *gracias* in return and got into the front seat of the taxi. Several of the men got into the back seat.

"Is this a taxi?" I asked.

"No taxi," said the driver.

"No taxi?"

He pulled away from the terminal, the car shaking like a blender. "Iquitos?" I questioned.

"*Si*, Iquitos."

"I want a taxi," I said in very bad high school Spanish. As I recall, I got a C in Spanish and had felt lucky to get it.

"No taxi Iquitos," I was told.

I looked out the window, and there didn't appear to be any taxis. Or buses. Maybe, like small towns everywhere, they were just being friendly. "*Gracias*" I said smiling all around. They all laughed at me.

It was only about six-thirty and the sun had already set. I was later to learn that it sets at six every night of the year. Groups of people seemed to be holding outdoor parties at the airport, and as we headed down a road that I hoped led to the town, families were gathered around fires on the sides of the road, cooking their dinners. Further on we passed small houses, or maybe shacks, that had no doors so that you could see inside. They appeared to have dirt floors and not much in the way of furniture, but practically every house had a television set and a motorcycle sitting in the middle of the one room. It looked like an interesting life-style.

As we headed into downtown Iquitos, I said to the driver, "Hotel."

"*Si*," he said, "hotel."

It occurred to me that maybe I should have made a reservation somewhere, but the woman at the information desk at the airport in Lima had told me the hotels were never full in Iquitos and it wouldn't be necessary.

The first thing that struck me about Iquitos was that there were very few cars; everyone was riding a motor scooter. In fact, it looked as though entire families were piled onto each small scooter, none of them wearing a helmet. There were also no stop signs or traffic lights. New York has always struck me as being the most anarchistic of American cities and Iquitos looked even more so.

The driver turned left off the main street and pulled up in front of a hotel. Everyone piled out of the car, got my trunk untied and carried my things into the lobby. When I held out some money to the driver, he smiled and shook his head and stuffed his hands into his pockets.

The hotel was built around a pool that was open to the sky. I was shown to a room on the second floor with a balcony that looked over the street. It had a double bed, a desk and chair, a Sony Trinitron and one twenty-watt bulb in the ceiling.

The smart thing to do would have been to have some dinner at the hotel and then get a good night's sleep. I hadn't come this far, though, not to find Sam as soon as possible. I took a shower with water that came out tepid no matter which faucet I turned, then changed into clean shorts and a T-shirt. People had laughed at my Banana Republic clothes and my safari hat all the way from Lima. I decided to save them for the jungle.

The clerk at the desk told me where to find the office of the Amazon Camp, which is the address where I wrote to Sam. It was on the main street, but about a half mile away from my hotel. I was excited as I set off. Just knowing I was in the same part of the world as Sam was giving me a natural high.

I finally spotted the Amazon Camp office on the other side of the street and crossed over. It was on a corner and open to the sidewalk on two sides. Inside, beneath a ceiling fan, one tall blond man was stretched out in a green leather chair, surrounded by shorter, darker men. They looked semi-enthusiastic at my approach.

One of the dark men, a boy really, got up and smiled at me. "Amazon tour, lady?"

"Maybe," I said.

The blonde signaled to one of the boys and he leaped out of his chair and offered it to me.

"I'm looking for Sam Wiley," I said.

"You a friend of his?" asked the blonde.

"I wouldn't have traveled this far if I weren't."

"I guess not," he said, nodding his appreciation of the fact that I had come a long way to see Sam.

"He gave me this as his address."

The blonde nodded. "I'm Paul Wright," he said. "I own this place."

"Iquitos?"

He grinned. "Not yet, but I'm working on it. And the way the economy's going down here, I might succeed."

"Is Sam around?"

"Sam's in the jungle," said Paul, "doing his thing. Although why anyone needs more than one movie of the jungle, I'll never know. I keep trying to get him to do a video for me for a promotional, but he's not interested."

"Could someone show me where he is?" I asked, not quite willing to go into the jungle unescorted.

"Tonight?" asked Paul.

"No, of course not. I'm not walking in there in the dark. Tomorrow morning?"

Paul turned to the boy who had given me his chair. "You busy tomorrow morning, Reniger?"

Reniger smiled at me in delight. "I take you to see Sam."

"How long a trip is it?" I asked, which, for some reason, got a big laugh.

"Are you asking how long it took Sam?" asked Paul.

"Well, I know he probably travels faster than I do," I said, picturing Sam fearlessly plowing through the dense vegetation.

"It took Sam three days," said Paul, and I could swear there was a twinkle in his eyes.

I must have turned pale at the news. Three days surrounded by foreign insects? I wasn't positive I loved Sam enough for that.

"I take you in motor boat," said Reniger.

"Reniger will get you there in a little over an hour," said Paul.

"Then why did it take Sam three days?"

Paul stroked his chin, his expression telling me that he was clearly enjoying this. "Well, to understand that, you have to understand Sam."

"I thought I did," I said.

Paul grinned. "Sam sees himself as some kind of explorer. He *likes* to rough it out hacking his way through the jungle. He'd probably be disappointed if he knew that he could've gotten there by boat."

"He doesn't know?"

"Oh, subconsciously I'm sure he does, but he won't admit it to himself. He must know that if he bathes in the Amazon, that it could also be used as transportation."

Paul said he'd arrange for Reniger to meet me there in the morning to carry my luggage down to the boat. I didn't have the guts to tell him I had a trunk with me.

THE TRIP up the Amazon was gorgeous. The sky was amazing. I wasn't used to skies that went on forever. The only time I ever saw the sky in New York was if I looked straight up. And since I walked looking down so as not to trip in a hole in the sidewalk, I rarely saw it at all. The river was low, making the water brown. It was pretty much uninterrupted jungle to our left, but on our right the jungle was broken up in spots by clusters of little houses and sometimes a cow or two.

The river was obviously the main road around there. We passed countless dugouts carrying entire families and sometimes livestock. Old women had umbrellas up to keep the sun off them. Many of the men wore baseball caps with the names of obscure American companies on them. The children waved to us.

Now that I had fearlessly flown down without being invited, I began to feel a little trepidation. What if I walked in on Sam living with a native woman? What if Sam wasn't happy to see me? What if Sam wasn't even there?

Six months ago I might have panicked at the situation. Now I only thought, *So what?* If any of those things transpired, I'd simply do a little souvenir shopping and then take the next flight back to New York. I loved Sam and I'd be sorry, but it wouldn't be the end of the world. Losing a man was never again going to be the end of the world for me. Nevertheless I found myself crossing my fingers.

At one point where the river branched, Reniger hung a left and then killed the motor and let the boat drift over to the shore. He jumped onto the land and then pulled the boat in so that I could get out without getting wet.

I looked for alligators and didn't see any. In fact I didn't even see a fish or an insect. I jumped onto the grass and helped Reniger unload my stuff. Then, with Reniger taking the lead with my trunk held on top of his head, I followed with my shoulder bag and suitcase.

I had pictured Reniger hacking his way through the jungle with a machete, but there was a nice path and it was easy going. It was cool inside the jungle, as not much sunlight penetrated. I was sure there were snakes and army ants and every other kind of fearful being, but I didn't see any. To my delight I did see a monkey that seemed to be grinning at me from one of the branches, and colorful parrots could be seen flying from tree to tree. I felt as if I was in some tourist attraction in Florida rather than in the Amazon jungle. Maybe you had to ease into it slowly for it to feel real. Maybe that was why Sam took the long route. All I knew was that a scant hour ago I was sitting over my second espresso in a restaurant that would have been at home on Columbus Avenue, and it was pretty hard now to switch to an intrepid explorer mode, particularly since the place was so civilized.

I saw Reniger shift the trunk off his head and set it down on the ground. I was about to tell him that I didn't need a rest, that it was a farther walk from my apartment house to the subway station, when I closed the gap between us and saw that we were in a clearing.

Sunlight streamed down on the remains of a campfire. Off to the right a striped hammock was set between

two trees. On a bamboo structure, raised about a foot off
the ground, were what looked to be Sam's supplies, covered by an olive-green rain poncho. Sam appeared to favor minimalistic decorating.

"You want me to look for Sam?" asked Reniger.

"No, that's okay. I'll just unpack and wait for him."

"You be okay on your own?"

"As long as there aren't any jungle animals lurking
about."

Reniger laughed. "Lots of monkeys," he said.

"I like monkeys."

"If you want to leave, just take the path back to the
river and wave to people in boats. Anyone give you a ride
to town."

"Thanks, Reniger," I said, admiring the way he wasn't
even sweating. I'd paid his fee to Paul and now I tried to
give him a few dollars, but he wouldn't take them.

"I see you later," he said, heading back down the path.

I opened my trunk and began to set out my goodies. I
had brought a special waterproof hammock with mos-
quito netting attached; a pillow and cotton blanket, as I
heard the jungle got cool at night, two deluxe Coleman
battery operated florescent lanterns, a folding camp
stove, a bright red canvas director's chair, a portable toilet and six rolls of toilet paper, a portable shower that
collected rainwater, a Sony cassette player and radio that
ran on solar energy, Malomars, Fig Newtons, Oreos,
crackers, cheese, peanut butter, a bottle of wine and
somewhat soft and squishy Godiva chocolates, a notebook and pen, a dozen paperbacks, last Sunday's *New
York Times*, and fifteen cans of insect repellant, which I
would spray on myself as soon as I saw a bug.

I arranged my home away from home at a distance
from Sam's in case, like Max, he liked his space. I tied my

hammock as well as I could, then set up everything else, using the trunk as a table. I constructed a sheet to go around the portable toilet, which I set at the far end of the clearing. When I was finished it looked quite cozy.

All it needed now was Sam.

IT WAS EARLY AFTERNOON when Sam walked into the clearing, loaded down with his camera equipment. I was sitting in my director's chair working on my next script. Alicia said she had run out of material about her life and suggested we do one on mine. The new script started out with a voice-over saying. "It was the summer the beaches died..."

I didn't hear him, as he trod lightly and I had a U2 tape playing in my cassette player. I sensed movement, though, and looked up to see Sam standing a few yards away from me. He cocked his head and gave me a level stare. I tried to assess his face for any indication of surprise or delight or even disgust. His face remained impassive as he glanced around, taking in my improvements to his camp.

When the silence between us thickened, I gave him a casual smile and said, "Hi, Sam."

He blinked as though he thought he was imagining me.

"How's your work going?" I asked him. I sensed that running and throwing myself into his arms was not the right approach. I had taken him totally by surprise and he needed time to adjust to it.

Sam moved a few feet closer, keeping me in his sight.

"Want an Oreo?" I asked, holding the package out to him.

Sam set his camera equipment down carefully, his eyes now on the Oreos. He wasn't in the desert so I didn't know why he was acting as though he was seeing a mirage.

"A glass of wine?" I offered. "I was just going to open the bottle. And if you wouldn't mind, would you check my hammock for me? I wanted to take a nap but I'm not at all sure my knots will hold."

"How . . . in hell . . . did you get here?"

"I flew."

He came a little closer. "How did you get through the jungle?"

I gave him my sunniest smile and lied. "I took the path."

"*What* path?"

"The path through the jungle."

"Carrying all this stuff?" he asked, waving his arms in the direction of my things and looking incredulous.

"Reniger helped me."

"Reniger."

"Paul loaned him to me."

"Paul."

I got up out of the chair and offered him a seat. "Sit down, Sam; you look like you need to."

Sam sunk slowly to the ground and sat cross-legged in the dirt.

I got the corkscrew and opened the bottle of wine. I poured him a glass and handed it to him. He seemed to be on automatic pilot as he took the glass and downed it. Not wanting him drunk, just relaxed, I didn't pour him another. He reached out and I was relieved when it was an Oreo he took, not the bottle.

He was still looking dazed. "You just show up, out of nowhere, in the middle of the jungle."

"What's the big deal?"

"You just get off an airplane and walk through the jungle until you find me."

"With help from Reniger."

"With help from Reniger."

"I thought perhaps you could use a little company."

"You don't call, you don't write..."

"I sent postcards and a care package."

"A casual acquaintance sends more than that."

"I don't recall getting any long letters from you."

"I'm not good at writing letters. I'm a visual person. I send pictures."

"Well, I did more than write—I stopped by to see you."

"I was afraid... Well, I was afraid maybe you got back together with Max."

That called for a drink. I poured myself a glass of wine and lifted it as I said, "I'm now officially divorced. I tried to think of a unique way of celebrating my single status, and I decided to come down here." I drank the wine, which was a bit warm for my taste. I guess you would call it room temperature, only the room temperature was in the nineties.

"Congratulations," said Sam, a little dazed, holding his glass out for more. I filled it halfway up, but he just sipped at it this time.

"Sam, how about telling me you're glad to see me? Of course if you're not glad to see me, I can always go back to Iquitos. My hotel there has air-conditioning, a lovely swimming pool and gets HBO on the TV." How it got HBO down there, I still hadn't figured out.

"I'm amazed to see you. In my wildest dreams I wouldn't have imagined you'd be in my camp when I got back."

I smiled. "You've been dreaming about me?"

"You could say that."

"Amazed doesn't do it," I said. "I want to hear happy. Delighted. Overwhelmed with emotion. A few tears would not be amiss."

Sam's face relaxed into a smile. "If you'd told me you were coming, I would've met you in town."

I shook my head. "Iquitos is too much like New York. I wanted to see you in your natural habitat. I figure, why come all the way down here and not see the jungle?"

"*Iquitos* is like *New York*?"

"The prices are lower, of course."

"I'm going to be back in New York in about six weeks."

"Call me impulsive."

He shook his head and grinned. "I've regretted more than once turning down your offer as my assistant."

"Really?"

He gave an admiring glance to my camp improvements. "And now that I see how comfortable you've made this place . . ."

"Yes?"

"Damn it, Ellie—not bringing you with me was one of the stupidest things I've ever done."

"That's lovely to hear."

"I've missed you like hell."

"That's even better."

"Do you forgive me?"

I smiled. "Better than that, Sam—I thank you."

"For what?"

"For not letting me be your assistant. Alicia pointed something out to me, and she was right. I didn't want to be your assistant, Sam—I wanted to be you. I envied you your life."

"We can share it."

"That's not enough anymore."

His smile faded. "I blew it, didn't I?"

I leaned forward and touched his face with my hand. "No, you didn't blow anything. Because of you, I've finally done something with my life. I'll never be satisfied to live vicariously again." I moved out of the chair and knelt in front of him. "Sam, I made my first documentary."

I saw the interest in his eyes when he said, "Are you serious?"

"Dead serious. I filmed Alicia. It's wonderful, Sam. We expanded it to ninety minutes and I intercut with shots of New York and the New Jersey shore. We just finished editing it—although Alicia did most of the editing—and we're entering it in some film festivals. We had a screening and everyone loved it."

"We're going to be competing," said Sam, but he sounded pleased about it.

"Yes. Isn't that wonderful?"

"I can't wait to see it."

"And I'm writing a new one."

"I'm not surprised. Those columns you sent me were wonderful."

"You liked them?" I felt so pleased by his praise I couldn't stop grinning.

"I damn near wore them out from reading them so many times." He put his hands on my shoulders and squeezed. "I can't think of any news that I would find quite so exciting. I'm proud of you, Ellie."

"And it's thanks to you."

"But I shafted myself in the process."

"I wouldn't say that."

Sam looked around the campsite again. "I don't get it. You bring all this stuff down here, I thought you were moving in."

"I figure I can stay ten days. That is, if you want me."

"You brought all this stuff for ten days?"

"I thought I'd bring you a little civilization. When I leave, you can toss it all."

"I don't know whether I'll let you leave."

"I'm not sure this is Sam Wiley I'm hearing."

"For the first time since I've been coming down here, I've been counting the days until I'll be back."

"Wait until you see my sublet."

"It was you I wanted to see."

"Nevertheless, it's air-conditioned and has a terrace. You're going to love it."

"Forget the apartment, do you have any idea how much I love you?"

"Well, you're in luck, because I still love you."

"I'm not giving up my work, you understand."

I laughed. "Neither am I."

"You don't mind a long-distance relationship for part of the year?"

"I think it sounds lovely."

"You're not supposed to say that. You're supposed to say that it's not perfect, but we can work things out."

"Oh, yes, I think we can work *anything* out."

Sam leaned forward and kissed the tip of my nose, then moved down to my waiting mouth. When we finally broke, he said, "Do you know what time it is?"

I looked at my watch. "Two o'clock."

"What're we doing sitting here? That's siesta time down here."

"Oh?"

"Want to join me in my hammock?"

I looked around.

"Don't worry, there's nobody within miles of us."

He stood up, then reached down and pulled me to my feet. As he folded me into his arms and we kissed, I thought that joining him in his hammock was about the best idea I'd ever heard.

As it turned out, it was even better than I'd imagined.

REVIEW
LOVE IN THE JUNGLE
by Ellie Thomas

Take a confirmed New Yorker, match her up with an adventurer hero, and what do you get? A steamy romance that makes *Romancing the Stone* look like Ma and Pa Kettle. The love scene in the hammock that ends up on the ground is so hot I'm surprised the film was only rated R. I have seldom seen two actors with the chemistry onscreen that these two have. In the scene where the two of them are swimming naked in the Amazon River the censors must have enjoyed it as much as I did and let it get through. Before they change their minds and cut it, get down to your local theater and pay your seven dollars. This one is worth every penny of it.

COMING IN OCTOBER

SWEET PROMISE

Erica made two serious mistakes in Mexico. One was taking Rafael de la Torres for a gigolo, the other was assuming that the scandal of marrying him would get her father's attention. Her father wasn't interested, and Erica ran home to Texas the next day, keeping her marriage a secret. She knew she'd have to find Rafael someday to get a divorce, but she didn't expect to run into him at a party—and she was amazed to discover that her "gigolo" was the head of a powerful family, and deeply in love with her....

Watch for this bestselling Janet Dailey favorite, coming in October from Harlequin.

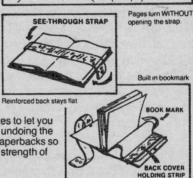